Clint knew it would all come down to Ted Singleton. He was the only one who knew all the players, and what side they were on. Clint had to find him in order to find the answers. Singleton had sent for him, so he must have still felt the bond of friendship and that Clint would be able to help him.

Clint had no intention of leaving Sacramento until he, too, knew all the players, knew where they stood, and knew what had happened to his friend.

And most of all, knew what the hell everybody was chasing . . .

THE GUNSMITH

303

TWO FOR TROUBLE

J. R. ROBERTS

JOVE BOOKS, NEW YORK

THE BERKLEY PUBLISHING GROUP
Published by the Penguin Group
Penguin Group (USA) Inc.
375 Hudson Street, New York, New York 10014, USA

Penguin Group (Canada), 90 Eglinton Avenue East, Suite 700, Toronto, Ontario M4P 2Y3, Canada
(a division of Pearson Penguin Canada Inc.)
Penguin Books Ltd., 80 Strand, London WC2R 0RL, England
Penguin Group Ireland, 25 St. Stephen's Green, Dublin 2, Ireland (a division of Penguin Books Ltd.)
Penguin Group (Australia), 250 Camberwell Road, Camberwell, Victoria 3124, Australia
(a division of Pearson Australia Group Pty. Ltd.)
Penguin Books India Pvt. Ltd., 11 Community Centre, Panchsheel Park, New Delhi—110 017, India
Penguin Group (NZ), 67 Apollo Drive, Mairangi Bay, Auckland 1311, New Zealand
(a division of Pearson New Zealand Ltd.)
Penguin Books (South Africa) (Pty.) Ltd., 24 Sturdee Avenue, Rosebank, Johannesburg 2196,
South Africa

Penguin Books Ltd., Registered Offices: 80 Strand, London WC2R 0RL, England

This is a work of fiction. Names, characters, places, and incidents either are the product of the author's imagination or are used fictitiously, and any resemblance to actual persons, living or dead, business establishments, events, or locales is entirely coincidental.

TWO FOR TROUBLE

A Jove Book / published by arrangement with the author

PRINTING HISTORY
Jove edition / March 2007

ISBN: 978-0-515-14266-2

JOVE®
Jove Books are published by The Berkley Publishing Group,
a division of Penguin Group (USA) Inc.,
375 Hudson Street, New York, New York 10014.
JOVE is a registered trademark of Penguin Group (USA) Inc.
The "J" design is a trademark belonging to Penguin Group (USA) Inc.

PRINTED IN THE UNITED STATES OF AMERICA

10 9 8 7 6 5 4 3 2 1

ONE

A summons to Denver usually meant that his friend Talbot Roper needed some help.

A request for his presence in Washington, D.C., invariably meant that his friend Jim West was going to drag him into some Secret Service affair he'd barely escape from with his life.

A telegram asking him to be in Sacramento at a certain time, in a certain place, was a mystery to Clint Adams. It seemed his willingness to help a friend had put his life in more jeopardy lately than usual. But he had set the precedent long ago, and it wasn't one he could break. Besides, if he didn't agree to help his friends, what would he be doing with his time? He certainly wasn't the type to sit and whittle, or settle down in a house or on a farm or—God forbid—behind the counter of a hardware or general store.

So here he was in Sacramento, registering at the Marsh House Hotel, having already left Eclipse at the nearest livery stable. He attracted attention walking from the stable to the hotel carrying his saddlebags, rifle and several pounds of trail dust on his clothes.

The telegram from Ted Singleton asked him to be in Sacramento and at the hotel on a certain day, so he had ridden hell-bent for leather from Labyrinth, Texas, to get there.

"Yes, sir," the desk clerk said, "we have your reservation right here. We've got you in the Presidential Suite."

"The Presidential Suite?"

"Yessir," the clerk said. "Second best accommodations in the hotel. Please sign here."

As Clint signed the register, he asked, "If the Presidential Suite is the second best room in the hotel, what's the best?"

"That would be Mr. Marsh's own suite, sir," the fastidious clerk said. "He is the owner."

"Well then," Clint replied, accepting his key, "I guess there's no harm in him having the best room in the hotel, is there?"

"No, sir," the clerk said, seriously. "There isn't."

Clint started to say he was kidding, but knew the clerk wouldn't get it.

"Much obliged," he said instead, and picked up his belongings.

"There are, uh, bathing facilities in the room, sir," the clerk hurriedly added.

"There are?" Clint asked. "And you're saying I need a bath?"

"I'm, uh, just making you aware, sir, of some of the hotel's amenities."

Again, Clint wanted to ask why the man hadn't told him about the restaurant, or barber station, but decided against it.

"Well," he said, instead, "thanks again."

He trudged up the stairs, bone weary, thinking that a bath didn't sound like a bad idea. The clerk probably just didn't want him sliding between the hotel's clean sheets until he'd had one.

As he entered the room, he gazed in appreciation around at the expensive furnishings, worthy of a Portsmouth Square hotel or whorehouse. But he wasn't in San Francisco, and these must have been the best accommodations not only in the hotel, but in town. Public accommodations, of course, Mr. Marsh's suite notwithstanding.

Actually, it was only the reason he was in Sacramento that was a mystery to Clint. Ted Singleton was an old lawman buddy who had retired from wearing the badge years ago. Clint hadn't heard from him in about five or six years, but that was no reason to ignore his call for help when it came . . .

"I could understand if it was Bat or Wyatt," Rich Hartman had said to him in Rick's Place, more than a week earlier. "Or even if it was me. How well do you know Singleton after all these years? Remember the mess you got into responding to that telegram from Colorado?"

"That one wasn't signed," Clint said, "this one is—and I knew Ted fairly well back then."

"Well, you don't know what kind of man he might have become since then," Rick said. "You've had friends go bad before."

"More than once," Clint agreed, "but I can't let that make me ignore them all."

"You're an amazing man when it comes to friendship, Clint," Rick said. "I guess I should count myself lucky I'm on the list."

"Yes," Clint Adam said to his friend, "you should . . ."

Clint's problem, he admitted to himself in private, was that his list of friends got longer and longer because he never crossed anyone off—unless they truly turned on him. And that had happened too few times for him to start crossing names off his list wholesale.

He almost tossed his saddlebags onto the bed, but they were dusty and the bed was so damn clean, he dropped them onto the floor instead. He leaned his rifle up against a chest of drawers.

The suite was two rooms, and he left the bedroom to go back out to the sitting room. Off to one side was another door, and when he opened it, he found the bath facilities. He could fill the tub with water himself, but he still had to call for help from downstairs to get hot water, and that was what he wanted.

He closed that door, walked over to the door of the room, opened that one and found himself looking down the barrel of a gun.

TWO

"Are you Clint Adams?" the woman asked from behind the gun.

Standing with his hands up around his shoulders, Clint said, "That's right."

"How do I know that?"

Clint studied the girl—and she was a girl, barely out of her teens, he thought. She was wearing boy's clothes, and the big Colt she was holding was already causing her wrist to bend a little.

"I don't know who you are," Clint said, "but I don't do well at the end of a gun."

"I know," she said. "According to your reputation, you're usually on the other end of a gun. Well, this time you're lookin' down my barrel—"

"Oh, what the hell," he said, and snatched the gun out of her hand.

She stared at him, mouth agape, and stammered, "You can't . . . How can you . . . How did you do that?"

Next he reached out, grabbed the front of her shirt and yanked her into the room, closing the door behind him. In doing so he pinched one of her peach-sized breasts beneath the shirt, and she grabbed it and said, "Ow!"

5

"I'm sorry," he said. "Didn't mean to do that."

"That hurt!"

"I said I'm sorry," he replied, then held the gun up and added, "but I didn't feel comfortable with you holding this."

"Give it back!"

"Later," he said, then added, "maybe."

She fell silent then, as if she suddenly realized where she was. She looked around with her mouth open, again.

"I have never been in such a room. It's . . . so big, and beautiful."

"It's very nice."

"What's out that window?" she asked, pointing.

"I don't know," he said. "I haven't had a chance to look."

"Can I?"

"Go ahead."

While she drew the curtain aside to gaze outside, he took the opportunity to unload the gun and put it down on a nearby table.

"It's the front of the hotel," she said. "I've never looked down at it like this. People going by, carriages . . ."

"Young lady, would you like to tell me your name?" he asked. "Just so I know what to call you?"

"I'm Julie," she said.

"That's it?"

She turned away from the window to face him.

"Just Julie."

"And why are you here?"

"Ted told me to come."

"Ted who?"

"You know," she said. "Singleton."

"You know Ted."

"Yes."

"Fat man, balding, mustache?" he asked.

"Tall, thin man, lots of gray hair, clean-shaven," she said. "You testin' me?"

"Yes."

"Did I pass?"

"Not yet," he said. "Why the gun?"

"I had to be sure."

"And are you?"

"The way you took that gun away from me?" she asked. "The speed of the way you moved? Oh yeah, you're the Gunsmith, all right."

"Now that we got that settled," he said, "what's your connection to Ted?"

"We work together."

"As what?"

"As partners."

"Partners . . . in what?"

"You know," she said, "partners. We work together, watch each other's back?"

"You watch Ted Singleton's back," he said, in disbelief.

"Well, of course," she said, as if he were an idiot. "That's what partners do, right?"

"Julie," he said, "stick with me here, all right?"

"Don't talk to me like I'm a child."

"I'm just a little confused," he said. "Can you just tell me what you and Ted are partners in?"

"You know," she said, and then lowered her voice, "we work for the government."

"The government?" he asked. "You and Ted work for the United States government?"

"Well, of course, silly," she said. "What other government would we work for?"

THREE

"Since when does Ted Singleton work for the government?" he asked. "And by 'government,' do you mean the Secret Service?"

"He's worked for them since I've known him," she said, "and I guess so."

"You guess so? You don't know for sure?"

"Well," she said, sheepishly, "I should say that Ted works for the government, and I work with Ted."

"So you only know what Ted tells you."

"Well . . . yeah. Why would he lie to me?"

Why indeed. The Ted Singleton he knew was not a liar, but as Rick Hartman had pointed out, people change. But why would Ted be lying to this young woman about working for the government? To get her into bed, maybe? Ted was a few years older than Clint, certainly too old to attract this girl under normal circumstances.

"So, Julie," Clint said, "just how close are you and Ted?"

The woman looked appalled.

"I know what you're suggesting, Mr. Adams," she said. "That's . . . terrible."

"I'm not suggesting anything," Clint said. "I'm just asking."

"Well don't," she said. "It's like I told you. We're just partners."

"Well, where is he?"

"That's the trouble," she said. "I don't know. I was hoping he'd come here to meet you."

"When's the last time you saw him?"

"Just after he sent you that telegram."

"And you haven't heard from him since?"

"Not a word."

Clint turned and walked away from her a few feet. When he turned back to say something, she was pointing a gun at him.

"Julie, that gun is empt—" he started to say, then realized it wasn't the same gun. The one he'd emptied was still on the table. This one was slightly smaller, not as heavy, and she'd had it hidden on her somewhere. It wasn't bending her wrist as much.

"What the hell?" he said.

"I'm sorry," she said, "but I have to be sure."

"About what?"

She hesitated a moment, then asked nervously, "Do you have it?"

"Do I have what?"

"Don't play games with me, Mr. Adams," she said. "Ted told me you were good friends. He's missing, and I'm thinkin' maybe he passed it on to you."

"I'll ask you again," Clint said. "Passed what on to me?"

She bit her lower lip and her eyes searched the room, as if she'd spot whatever "it" was that she was talking about.

"Julie . . . if that's your real name . . ."

"It is."

"I don't know what you're talking about," he said. "I haven't seen Ted. I just got here a little while ago. He didn't leave anything for me, and I don't know what 'it' is you're talking about."

She looked as if her feet were nailed to the floor, she was so unsure of her next move.

"Why don't you put down the gun and we can talk—" he started.

"N-no," she said. "I gotta go. Back up."

He took a step back.

"More!"

He took two steps back. She came forward and collected her other gun from the table.

At the door she said, "If you see Ted, tell him I'm lookin' for him."

"You should stay here, Julie, so we can work together on finding him."

"I gotta go," she said. "Gotta go."

She had the big Colt stuck awkwardly into her belt, and the other gun still in her left hand. With her right, she opened the door, and without another word, she stepped out and pulled the door closed behind her.

He thought about going after her, but in her agitated state she might take a shot at him. Instead he went to the window to see when she hit the street. It only took a few moments and there she was. She had put her gun away and was hurrying across the street.

She hesitated there, looked up at his window. He didn't know if she could see him, but he didn't step back at all. She watched a few more moments, then turned and hurried up the street.

He dropped the curtain back into place and left the window.

FOUR

Clint had his bath, after making sure his door was locked and a chair was slid under the doorknob. He didn't want Julie sneaking back in with her guns. He took the bath quickly, because the water was cold, but afterward he felt refreshed.

His telegram from Singleton had said only that he should check into the hotel and wait to be contacted. Now he wondered if that meant contacted by someone other than Singleton himself. And if Julie really worked with Ted, why hadn't it been her?

He couldn't imagine Singleton actually being partnered with the young woman, so the liar had to be Julie. Somehow she knew that Ted had contacted him, and knew he was coming to Sacramento to register in this hotel. But on top of all that, she obviously thought that Singleton was going to give him . . . "it." Whatever it was.

Clint got dressed, thought about leaving his gunbelt behind in favor of his little New Line Colt, but in the end he strapped the gunbelt on. After all, someone had already pointed two guns at him.

Clint decided he'd wonder about Ted Singleton later. If

the girl was a liar, then Singleton was still going to contact him. Until he did, he was going to go out and have a steak.

The woman across the restaurant kept looking at him.

She was a dark-haired beauty in her thirties, dining alone. He had noticed her as soon as he walked in, and she had apparently noticed him at the same time. Neither of them had been served dinner yet, so Clint decided to make a bold move. What could it hurt? He had nothing else to do.

He called the waiter over and said, "Would you ask the lady over there if I could join her?"

"Mrs. Tate?" the man asked.

"Is that her name?"

The balding waiter nodded and said, "Yessir."

"Does she eat here often?"

"Quite often."

"Alone?"

"Almost all the time."

"Does she live in town?"

"I think she's staying at a nearby hotel, sir," the waiter said. "She's been in here every night for about a week, but before that I had never seen her."

"Well, before our dinners come, would you ask her if I can join her, or if she would like to join me?"

"Of course, sir," the waiter said, "and if she asks for your name?"

"Adams," Clint said, "my name is Clint Adams."

"Yessir," the waiter said. "I'll extend your invitation."

"Thank you."

Apparently, Mrs. Tate had decided to be bold herself. As soon as the waiter spoke to her, she reacted immediately. She stood up and walked across the room to Clint's table. He saw that she was tall, full-figured, and as she got closer, he put her age at close to forty—but a beauty nonetheless.

"Mr. Adams?"

He stood and said, "That's right."

She smiled and extended her hand.

"Amanda Tate."

"Mrs. Tate," he said, taking her hand. "Will you join me?"

"I certainly will," she said. "I hate eating alone, and I have been doing it for days."

"Please," he said, "have a seat." As she did, he asked, "Can I get you a drink?"

"May we have champagne?" she asked.

"I don't see why not," he said. She was a woman of expensive tastes, but he didn't mind.

He called the waiter over and ordered a bottle of champagne. The man fetched it, opened it at the table and poured them each a glass.

Amanda Tate raised hers and said, "To new friendships."

"And exquisite beauty," he added.

"Thank you, sir."

They clinked glasses and drank.

"How long have you been in Sacramento, Mr. Adams?" she asked.

"I just arrived today," he said, "and my name is Clint."

"I'm Amanda."

"Now that we have that settled—" he said. But before he could finish, the waiter arrived with their dinners. As he set the plates down on the table, Clint saw that she had ordered the same thing, steak dinner with all the trimmings.

"I see we have something in common already," she said, staring him straight in the eyes. "This night might not be as boring as I had feared."

FIVE

Naked, her pale breasts were like overripe melons, sagging just a bit as a concession to age. He stripped her down in the center of the room, then lifted each breast to his mouth, first licking the nipples until they were hard and then sucking them into his mouth.

Amanda sighed and let her head drop back as Clint concentrated his efforts on her breasts. Her nipples were brown, with wide aureoles, and he spent a lot of time on them, squeezing her breasts while he sucked on her, thoroughly enjoying the way the weight felt in his hand, the way her nipples felt in his mouth as he sucked and chewed on them.

Finally, she couldn't stand it anymore and she pushed him away, gasping.

"Take off your clothes," she demanded.

He smiled at her and said, "You take them off."

He did remove his gunbelt himself, and hung it on the bedpost within easy reach, but he left the rest of his clothes for her to remove.

She eagerly divested him of his clothing until he was only in his underwear. She fell to her knees and peeled those off slowly, until his rigid cock sprang into view. She caught her breath with what sounded like "Um," then tugged the shorts down to his feet so he could kick them away. Then she took hold of him and pressed him to her soft cheek, rubbed the hot column of flesh all over her face and finally slid her tongue out to taste him. She cupped his balls and licked his shaft, wetting him fully, then opened her mouth to take him in. She sucked him slowly at first, causing him to tense and go up onto his toes. Then her tempo increased and he began moving his hips in unison, and was as much fucking her mouth as she was sucking him.

When she felt that he was close, she released him from her mouth with an audible pop and pushed him back onto the bed. She crawled up onto it with him, straddled him, and mounted him. As every inch of him sank into her steamy depths, they both sighed, and then began to move together. She rode him hard, her big breasts swaying in his face until he grabbed them, squeezed them together and sucked both nipples at the same time.

She gasped, her eyes widening, and began to ride him even faster and harder, and he knew she was chasing her orgasm. He took up the chase with her, hoping they'd catch it at close to the same time . . .

Clint woke with a gun in his face. Holding the gun was Amanda Tate, who was sitting in a chair—still naked—next to the bed.

"Was I that bad?" he asked.

"Where is it, Clint?"

He pushed himself up into a seated position on the bed. His gunbelt was still on the bedpost, but he didn't want to kill this woman, anymore than he'd wanted to kill Julie.

"What 'it' are we talking about, Amanda?" he asked her.

"You know."

"No, I'm afraid I don't know."

The gun she was holding looked like a .32 Colt Patterson, not too big for her, and she held it very steady. She had her knees pulled up so that her breasts were hidden, but that wasn't the point of the position. She was just comfortable in her skin.

"Then why are you here?"

"Okay," he said, "the questions have to become more clear. Why am I here with you? Here in this hotel? Or here in Sacramento?"

"All three."

"Well," he said, "why I'm here with you is obvious, I think. I mean, just look at you."

She actually smiled and said, "Thank you."

"Why I'm here in this hotel, and in Sacramento, is to meet my friend Ted Singleton."

"So you admit you know him?"

"Yes, I know him," he said. "I haven't seen him in five or six years, but I know him."

"And you haven't seen him since you arrived?"

"No."

"And he didn't leave something for you?"

"No."

"Something to hold?"

"No."

"Or hide?"

"No. Are these the right answers?"

"To tell you the truth, I'm not sure."

"It would help me if I knew what he was supposed to have left me," he said. "Then, at least, when people stick guns in my face, I'll know why."

"Someone else has stuck a gun in your face?"

"Yes."

"Since you got here?"

"Yes."

"Who?"

Clint saw no reason to lie about any of this. At least, not until he heard something from Ted Singleton.

"A girl named Julie."

"Julie who?"

"I don't know," he explained. "All I got was Julie. She claims she works with Ted. Do you know Ted, by the way?"

"I know him," she said, "and I don't know anything about him working with anyone."

"Not even you?"

"Ted and I are working at cross purposes," she said, "I can tell you that."

"So you're working against the government?" he asked her.

"What? No, of course not," she said, as if he was crazy. "I work for the government."

"Secret Service?"

"Another branch."

"But secret?"

"Yes."

"So you can't tell me who you work for."

"Right."

"And you won't tell me what 'it' is."

"If you don't already know," she said, "you're safer not knowing at all. Believe me."

"I'd believe you, if you were to put that gun down."

She looked at the gun in her hand as if she'd just re-membered it, then shrugged and set it aside on the table next to the bed.

"I'm sorry about that," she said. "I just had to be sure."

"And you are?"

"I don't think you'd lie to me," she said. "Besides, you could have drawn your gun anytime and shot me. After all, you are the Gunsmith."

"So you were testing me?"

She unfolded her beautiful body and crawled back onto the bed with him.

"Let's just say I was . . . well, yeah, testing you."

"So if I'd failed the test," he said, "you'd be dead now."

She scratched her head.

"Guess I didn't think of it that way." She leaned into him, putting her head on his shoulder and her hot body against his. "Do you want me to leave?"

"Just because you pointed a gun at me?" he asked, reaching for her. "Not a chance."

SIX

At breakfast the next morning in the hotel dining room, Clint once again tried to get Amanda Tate to tell him who she worked for and what "it" was.

"How am I going to know it if I don't know what it is?" he asked.

"And what would you do if you found it, Clint?" she asked. "Give it to me or to Ted Singleton?"

She had him there.

"Ah, you hesitated," she said.

"I'd have to talk to Ted first, Amanda," he said. "Find out his side."

Around a piece of bacon, she said, "I'm telling you he's the wrong side, and I'm the right side."

"I'm sorry, but I just can't take your word for that. He's my friend."

"Aren't I your friend since last night?"

"Are you here from Washington, D.C.?" he asked.

"What makes you ask that?"

"You have neither a Western nor a Southern accent," he said. "I'm trying to figure out where you're from."

"Never mind," she said. "You didn't seem to care where I was from last night in your bed."

23

"Everybody knows that when a man and a woman are in bed together," Clint explained, "the bed is neutral territory."

"Everybody knows that?"

"Everybody who's ever been in bed with a woman . . ."

". . . or a man," she finished.

"That's right."

She put down her knife and fork and stared at him. She was either sincere, or very good at appearing sincere.

"Believe me, Clint, I would tell you if I could," she said. "Last night I just had to find out if you'd seen Singleton."

"And what are you going to do today?"

"Try to track him down."

"Let me come along."

"Oh . . . I can't do that."

"I can help," he said. "I know how he thinks."

"You know how Ted Singleton used to think," she said. "You don't know the man now."

"And you do?"

"Yes."

"Then you tell me," Clint said, "where is he? Why did he send for me?"

"I don't know," she said, "but I'm going to find out. How long will you be in Sacramento?"

"Until I find out what happened to Ted."

She put her silverware down and leaned forward.

"Just stay here at the hotel today until you hear from me, Clint," she said. "I really am the one with the best chance of finding him. You don't know the city."

"I've been here before, Amanda."

"That may be, but you still don't know it as well as I do."

He couldn't fault her there. It had been a while since he'd been there last, and even then there was a lot of the city he'd never seen.

But he still didn't intend to just stay at the hotel and wait—but he didn't tell her that.

"All right, then," he lied. "I'll wait to hear from you."

"Good."

"What do I do if you don't come back?"

"After last night?" she asked. "Believe me, Mr. Adams, I'll be back."

SEVEN

After Amanda left, Clint paid the check and went in search of a telegraph office. He stopped at the front desk to ask the clerk where the nearest one was.

"Two blocks east, sir," the young man said. "You can't miss it."

Clint missed it, had to turn around and come back to find it, but finally did. He sent a telegram to Washington, D.C., to his friend Jim West, who was a Secret Service agent. He didn't want to name names, but he indicated there were some people in Sacramento claiming to be agents, and asked if West knew of anyone who might actually be there, in the city, working for the United States government in any capacity?

He left the name of the hotel he was staying in and asked the clerk to send over any reply extraquick. He gave him some extra money, above and beyond the word count money, and told him there would be more when the reply was delivered.

"Yes, sir," the man said. "You'll have it as soon as it arrives."

He left the telegraph office and stood out on the street in front for a few moments. He had considered following

Amanda today, but she had taken that decision away from him. He'd followed her outside, but she had already disappeared. If she was actually working for the government, she was good. If not . . . well, she was still good.

With the telegram sent, he decided he was stuck doing just what Amanda had suggested he do: stay around his hotel. For one thing he had to wait for the reply from Washington, and for the other he had to be there when Amanda came back.

Was she coming back? With any word about Ted Singleton? That remained to be seen. And what about Julie? Where and when would she turn up next, if at all?

Heading back to his hotel, he briefly considered checking hospitals to see if Ted Singleton was in any of them, but then he dismissed that.

When he'd known Singleton, the man had been a star packer. He'd worn a badge for over thirty years. Surely that was the kind of man a government agency might want to recruit, but the problem with that was Singleton had always hated anything federal. He'd always said he'd never wear a federal marshal's badge, because all marshals were pricks. It was the town sheriffs, he claimed, who upheld the law and did all the work.

Of course, being a member of the Secret Service was nothing like being a federal marshal.

Or—as far as Singleton would be concerned—was it?

"Where have you been?"

Ben Avery looked up from his cards as Amanda Tate entered the small saloon.

"You mean today?" she asked. "Or last night?"

"I mean ever," Avery said. "You just disappeared for a while."

"Well, I'm back," she said. "Buy a girl a drink?"

Avery looked over at the bartender and nodded, meaning Amanda could have whatever she wanted. He didn't own the small saloon, but he had that kind of influence in the small place.

"Brandy," Amanda said.

The bartender poured and handed it to her, and she carried it back to the table to sit across from Avery.

"Black nine on the red ten."

"Thanks."

"Do you know who Clint Adams is?"

"I haven't spent my life under a rock, Mandy," Avery said. She hated that name, but she couldn't get him to stop using it. "We talkin' about the Gunsmith?"

"In the flesh." Of course, he had no idea of the pun involved.

"Why are we talkin' about him?"

"He's in Sacramento."

Avery stopped looking at his cards and looked at her.

"What is he doin' here?

"Looking for Ted Singleton."

Now Avery put the cards down.

"Why?"

"They're friends."

"Why would he be here lookin' for him now?" Avery asked.

"Because Ted sent for him."

Avery rubbed his hands over his face. At twenty-eight he was more than a few years younger than she was, but she deferred to him. He was well dressed, well scrubbed, well appointed. He had the cleanest hands of any man she had ever known . . . but that was just physically.

His charcoal gray suit was wrinkled, as if he'd had it on since yesterday, or longer. His tie was gone, probably in his pocket. She knew he had a .32 Colt, much like hers, in a shoulder rig under his left arm.

"Is he stayin'?"

"Yes."

"How long?"

"Until he finds or hears from Ted Singleton."

"Well then," Avery said, "maybe he should."

"See him?" Amanda asked. "How do you plan on arranging that?"

"No, not see him," Avery said. "Maybe he should get a message from him."

"Delivered by whom?"

He smiled at her and asked, "Who else?"

She sipped her brandy.

"Where is he?"

"At his hotel." She told him which one. "He said he'd wait there to hear from me."

"And will he?"

"I think so."

"Did he follow you?"

"No, Ben," she said. "I know when I'm being followed."

"Don't get testy," he said. "I'm just askin'."

"No, he didn't follow me."

"Well then, I guess we better get to it."

"Get to what?"

"Composin' a message for him that he'll believe. How well does he know Ted?"

"Knew him well, but hasn't seen him for five or six years."

"A lot can happen to a man in five or six years," Avery said.

"Yes, it can."

"Well," Avery said, "you know Ted better than anyone. Come up with somethin'."

"What about the girl?" Amanda asked. "She went to see the Gunsmith, too."

"What'd she do?"

"Stuck a gun in his face."

"That shouldn't have fazed a man like him."

"It didn't," she assured him.

"How much does he know?"

"Nothing," she said. "Not a blessed thing, or so he claims."

"And you believed him?"

"Yes."

"Why?"

She smiled. "Let's just say he was in no position to lie to me."

EIGHT

Clint decided to make it easy for anyone who wanted to find him—Amanda, the telegraph clerk or even Ted Singleton. He got himself a chair and set himself down out in front of the hotel.

Maybe even the girl, Julie, would want to come back and talk to him. She interested him even more than Amanda did. He still couldn't imagine that Singleton would work with such a young, obviously inexperienced girl. There must have been some other reason she thought they were partners, and that he worked for the government.

What was she doing at that moment? he wondered. Wandering the streets, looking for Singleton? Or was she looking for the elusive, mysterious "it"?

Clint wondered what "it" was, but that didn't really matter when it came right down to, uh, well, it. What he was more interested in was Ted Singleton himself.

Where was Ted, what had happened to him not only in the last few days, but the past few years, what kind of man was he now? What was his relationship with the two women, Julie and Amanda?

Clint tried to recall Ted's general attitude toward women. He had never gotten married, never talked much about women. Mostly, when they drank together, he would talk about the law and what it meant to him. Now that he thought about it, Singleton never talked much about women because it was the law that he loved. The law that had been his mistress for many years.

How, Clint wondered, did he feel about his mistress now?

The telegraph operator put down his pencil and read the message again, then picked up the pencil and hurriedly copied it word for word onto another slip of paper. He folded that paper and put it in one pocket, then picked up the telegram and left the office, heading for the Marsh House Hotel.

Clint saw the telegraph operator coming down the street toward him and decided to remain in his chair until the man reached him.

"Got that reply you was waitin' for," the man said, holding it out.

Clint noticed that the man's hand was shaking. It might have been normal for him, except that Clint had not noticed it the first time they'd talked. He did not immediately take the telegram.

"Are you nervous?" he asked.

"Uh, no, sir."

"Why is your hand shaking?"

"Um, it does that, sometimes."

"You know," Clint said, sitting back in his chair, bringing the front legs up off the walk, leaving the man to continue holding the telegram out, "I have always wondered about telegraph operators."

"Wondered what . . . sir?"

"Well, all the messages you write down all day long," Clint said, "with nobody around to watch you? What's to stop you from making some copies?"

"Copies?"

"You know," Clint said, "taking your little pencil and writing another copy."

"Um." The man scrunched up his face, still, for some reason, holding his hand out. "Why would I do that, sir?"

"Do you know who I am?"

"Well, your name was on your telegram."

"But do you know who I am?"

"Well . . . yes, sir."

Clint decided to stop beating around the bush. He brought the front legs of his chair down hard.

"What's your name?"

"P-Philip, sir."

Philip looked to be in his thirties, a dapper little man with a fussy mustache and garters on his sleeves.

"Philip, you're just too damn nervous for my taste," Clint said. "I think you copied that telegram you're holding onto another piece of paper, and I think you have it in your pocket. Give it to me."

For a moment Philip looked as if he was going to cry.

"Sir—Mr. Adams—I didn't—"

"Hand it over." Clint snatched away the telegram the operator had been holding out for minutes now. The man's arm must've felt like it was going to fall off. Instead of pulling it back quickly, he drew it back slowly.

"Come on, Philip," Clint said. "Don't make me have to search you."

Slowly, the clerk reached into his pocket and brought out the folded piece of paper. He held it out to Clint, who took this one right away.

"So you sell information when you think it might be worth something to you?"

"Yessir," Philip said. "If you won't tell my boss, though—I mean, I'd get fired—"

"And then you'd have no job, and no information to sell."

"No, sir."

"Well, I don't see any reason that your boss has to know . . ."

"Oh, thank you, sir."

". . . as long as you tell me one thing."

"What's that, sir?" Philip asked, suspiciously.

"Who were you going to sell this information to?" Clint asked.

"Oh, sir, please—"

"Somebody you're afraid of?"

"Y-yes."

"More afraid of than you are of me?"

"W-well—"

Clint leaned forward so he was almost nose to nose with the smaller man.

"I think you should be more afraid of me, Philip," he said, slowly. "Don't you? At least, at this moment."

"Um, y-yessir."

"Then give me a name," Clint said, "and tell me where to find the person. Then you can go and keep your job, and keep your profitable little sideline going."

Reluctantly, Philip gave him a name.

NINE

Clint was glad for the telegraph operator's nerves. He was now armed with the name of a man who might have paid for the information that the Gunsmith was in town. Also for the fact that the Gunsmith had sent a telegram to Washington, D.C. The telegram in reply to which Jim West told him that he knew of no Secret Service people in Sacramento at that time.

Victor Barrett was what big cities had started to call a "crime boss." He was in charge of everything from prostitution to drugs to "loan-sharking"—another new term—in most of Sacramento, according to Philip, the telegraph operator. And he paid well for information he thought was worth paying for. To that end, he papered the whole city with bribe money so that information flowed to him from every corner.

Now Victor Barrett was going to get more than just information about Clint Adams. He was going to get Clint Adams in person.

Clint was glad for the clerk's nerves, because without them he never would have known about Barrett, who was the kind of man who might be able to tell him what this elusive "it" was that everyone in Sacramento was chasing.

Well, maybe not everyone . . .

• • •

Victor Barrett liked the docks. He'd grown up there, working them beside his father until the old man had keeled over dead while they were loading a freighter—or was it unloading? He didn't remember, he just knew that his father died on the docks, and since he'd hated the old codger, he loved the docks for freeing him.

Once his father was dead, Victor began to move up. His father had always held him back, telling him how honest dock work was and how well it paid. Yeah, Victor thought, and it also broke your back and made you old before your time. That was not the life for him.

Victor made connections in his teens, worked for powerful men until he got old enough to become powerful himself. The men he'd stepped on—or killed—on his way up were gone. Victor Barrett was now *the* powerful man in Sacramento. Thugs, honest men, lawyers, judges, politicians, even lawmen came to him for favors, and waited anxiously to learn whether or not he was going to grant them.

He chose to live on the docks, in an apartment above a bar he owned. The bar was the first thing he had bought when he'd earned enough money to start owning things— buildings, and people.

Victor Barrett was thirty-two and, to his mind, the most powerful, most feared man in Sacramento. Everybody kowtowed to him. The Chinks, the Micks, the Wops, the Niggers, the Whites . . . everybody.

Of course, Barrett had no way of knowing—or no capacity for believing—that the bulk of the population of Sacramento had never heard of him. That was something he'd never want to be told, that people, who lived in their homes, went to and from work every day and led quiet, productive, private lives, had never heard of him. But to the men and women who populated his little crime world, he was king.

At this moment the king was sitting on his throne—a chair at a back table in the Docksider Tavern. Barrett preferred to word "tavern" to "saloon." He'd heard it from sailors for years, and when he bought the place, he decided that was what he was going to call it—a tavern.

When the front door to his tavern opened, and the tall, well-built man wearing a sidearm came in, he noticed him right away. Most men who entered his place didn't wear guns in plain sight. So this man was unusual. He was obviously a stranger, who didn't know where he was.

Victor decided to watch.

Clint walked into the Docksider and stopped just inside the door. It was about a quarter full; all the men looked like dockworkers, and there were no guns in sight. That didn't mean there were none in the room, though.

He walked to the bar, aware that he was being watched. Some of the men were following him with their eyes idly, mostly for something to do. There was one man, though, who was watching him for different reasons. He was fairly certain this was Victor Barrett.

"Help ya?" the barkeep asked.

"Beer."

The bartender drew one and sloppily placed it on the bar in front of Clint, sloshing some of it over onto the bar's surface.

"Anything else?"

Clint stared down at the dirty mug of beer—or mug of dirty beer, he couldn't be sure.

"Yeah," Clint said. "Victor Barrett."

The bartender inclined his head toward the back of the room, confirming what Clint had thought, that the man in the back was Barrett.

"Do I need an appointment?"

The bartender looked over at Barrett, and the two actually seemed to be able to communicate without speaking.

"You got an appointment," the bartender said. "Now."

"Thanks."

Clint turned to walk back.

"Don't ferget yer beer."

"Oh," Clint said, "yeah, thanks."

He hesitated, but picked up the mug and carried it to the back with him.

TEN

"Have a seat."

Clint sat opposite Victor Barrett, who didn't feel the need to introduce himself.

"My name is Clint Adams."

Barrett's eyebrows went up.

"I know the name." He looked over at the bartender and waved. "Let me get you a good mug of beer."

By "good" Clint figured the man meant clean. The bartender appeared very quickly with a clear mug of beer, nothing floating in it or coating the sides of the mug.

"Such a special guest requires a clean glass," Barrett said.

"Thanks."

Clint was surprised by Barrett's youth. He didn't know the man's reputation; he only knew what the telegraph clerk had told him, which wasn't much. He also knew the fact that the clerk had been very frightened of the man.

"What brings the famous Gunsmith not only to Sacramento, but to my place?' Barrett asked.

"It's come to my attention that you're a man who knows what's going on in this town."

"I have that reputation."

"I was wondering if you'd consider helping me out."

Barrett sat back, hooked his thumbs into his maroon vest.

"Why would I want to do that, Mr. Adams?"

"I actually have no idea, Mr. Barrett," Clint said, "but I thought there was no harm in asking."

Barrett stared at Clint and smiled.

"You've got a lot of nerve, you know that?" he asked. "But then, you're a legend of the West, right? I guess you didn't achieve your reputation without a certain amount of guts."

"I'll tell you what," Clint said. "You help me out and I'll owe you a favor."

"You're not gonna offer me any money for this service?"

"In your position," Clint said, "I wouldn't think you'd need my money. I mean, I can't offer you the kind of bribe you're used to."

"Actually," Barrett said, "I pay out more bribes than I bring in."

"Really?" Clint asked. "That doesn't seem like good business to me."

Barrett frowned and said, "No, me neither."

"So will you help me?"

Barrett still seemed lost in thought for a moment, then shook his head and focused on Clint.

"I tell you what," he said. "Since I've never had a legend in my place before, I'm gonna help you out—if I can."

"Well, I appreciate that."

"Now, what seems to be the problem."

"I'm looking for a friend of mine," Clint said. "His name is Ted Singleton."

"And what makes you think I know who he is, or where he is?"

"Well, people with guns—women, in fact—keep sticking their guns in my face and asking me where he is."

"I can think of something I'd rather have women stick in my face other than guns," Barrett said.

"So can I. But they're also asking me a funny question."

"What's that?"

"Where is it?"

"Where is what?"

"No," Clint said, "that's the question they keep asking me. 'Where is it?'"

"And do you know what 'it' is?" Barrett asked.

"I don't have a clue."

"Then I guess you also don't know where 'it' is?"

Clint shook his head.

"And you think I do?"

"I think," Clint said, "from what little I've been told about you, if there's an 'it' in Sacramento that's worth something, you'd know what it is."

"I'm flattered," Barrett said. "Who's been talkin' about me?"

"One of your informants," Clint said. "I don't want to say who. He's kind of afraid of you. Thinks he'll end up in the water if you find out he was talking to me."

"He's probably right," Barrett said. "What can you tell me about your friend Singleton?"

"You don't know him?"

"Would I be askin' you who he is if I did?"

Clint took the time to tell Barrett about the Ted Singleton he knew.

"Sounds like he was a pretty straight arrow," Barrett said.

"'Was' is the right word," Clint said. "I don't know if he's changed since then."

Barrett rubbed the bridge of his nose with his right forefinger. Some people in Sacramento had come to recognize the gesture. Clint, never having met Barrett before, could not.

"I'll see what I can find out, Mr. Adams," Barrett finally said. "Where are you staying?"

"The Marsh House."

"Nice hotel."

"It's okay. Like I said, too many women with guns are finding their way into my room."

"And who are these women?"

Clint hesitated, then replied, "I don't think I want to tell you that, just yet."

"As you wish," Barrett said. "All right, sit tight at your hotel and I'll be in touch."

Funny, Amanda Tate had told him essentially the same thing.

Clint stood up. His beer remained on the table, untouched.

"Thanks for your time," he said.

Barrett surprised him by leaning forward and extending his hand. The two men shook.

"Pleasure's mine," Barrett said. "Truth is I've read a lot about you. You're sort of an idol of mine."

Clint didn't know what to say to that. Finally he said, "I guess I'm flattered."

"I'll be in touch," Barrett said, again.

As Clint left the tavern, the bartender came over and said, "He didn't drink his beer."

"Smart man," Barrett said. "I wouldn't drink the beer here, either, if I didn't own the joint."

The barkeep picked up the mug. He'd seen Barrett rub his nose, and he knew what it meant.

"You got a plan?"

"I got somethin'," Barrett said. "I'm gonna need Jerry and Roman."

"I'll find them."

Barrett nodded. The bartender went back to the bar. Barrett lit up one of his buck-a-piece cigars, leaned back and puffed on it. He didn't have a plan yet, but he'd have one soon. First, he was going to have to find out what this elusive and in demand "it" was.

Couldn't have an "it" like that lying around Sacramento without him knowing about . . . it.

ELEVEN

Clint went back to his hotel. He figured he'd done all he could for the moment. Going to Victor Barrett on the word of the telegraph operator had been a long shot. Maybe first thing the next morning he should go to the law, check Barrett out for himself. He wouldn't have to tell them about Julie and Amanda and Singleton—not yet, anyway.

When he got back to the Marsh House, he checked at the desk for messages and was told there were none.

"Thanks," he said, and started to walk off.

"There was somebody here lookin' for you, though," the young clerk said.

"Oh? Who?"

"Didn't leave her name."

"A woman?"

"Yes, sir," the clerk said, emphasis on the word "sir."

That probably meant it was Amanda—unless the clerk preferred young women like Julie.

"What'd she look like?"

"A woman, sir," the clerk said. "A real woman."

"Young?"

"Not so young," the clerk said, "but that don't matter, right?"

47

It was Amanda.

"Dark-haired?"

"Yes, sir," the clerk said, "and, if you don't mind me sayin' so, a very womanly figure on her."

"No," Clint said, "I don't mind. She didn't leave a message? You're sure?"

"She seemed real put out that you weren't here, sir," he said. "No message."

"Did she say she'd be back?"

"She said something I wouldn't expect to come out of a lady's mouth, sir," the clerk answered, "but she didn't say whether she'd be back or not."

"Okay, thanks."

Clint was about to go up to his room when he thought of one more question for the young clerk.

"One more thing," he said.

"Sir?"

"She didn't bribe you to let her into my room, did she?"

"Well, sir . . ." The man looked sheepish.

"She's up there now?"

"Yes, sir—you won't tell my boss, will you, sir? I'd get fired, for sure."

Clint had never had so many jobs in the palm of his hand.

"No," he said, "I'm not going to tell your boss."

He headed up to the room.

Amanda Tate made herself comfortable in Clint's suite. She'd never stayed in such a room before—not by herself, anyway. There was a time in her life when she'd been sent to rooms like this for the pleasure of the man who was renting it. She decided to enjoy the room until Clint Adams came back, maybe even pretend like it was hers.

She poured herself some brandy and walked around, touching everything—the expensive furnishings, the flocked wall coverings, the glass fixtures. She was pouring herself a second brandy from the crystal decanter when she heard the key in the lock. She thought about taking out her gun, but decided she wouldn't need it. The Gunsmith had already proven he couldn't resist her charms.

She seated herself in one of the expensive, overstuffed chairs, holding her brandy snifter in one hand, the other beneath her chin.

Posing.

Waiting.

TWELVE

As Clint entered, he saw Amanda sitting, waiting, with a glass of brandy. Thankfully, there was no gun pointing at him.

"Hello, Amanda," he said, closing the door behind him.

"Where have you been?" she demanded. "You were supposed to wait to hear from me."

"I got bored," he told her. "I went for a walk."

"Hope you don't mind," she said, raising the glass, "I helped myself . . . twice."

"That's the hotel's booze, not mine," he said, "and I'm not paying the tab here, anyway—at least, I don't think I am."

It was a good question. Had Ted Singleton paid the bill in advance, and if not, would he be around to pay it when Clint checked out?

"That's neither here nor there," Amanda said. Clint wasn't sure what that meant. "Do you want a drink?"

"No, thanks," he said. "Do you have any news for me about Ted?"

"I have a message."

"To who?"

"To you," she said. "Who else?"

"He sent me a message? In writing?" Would he remember what Ted's handwriting looked like? Probably not.

"No, not in writing," she said. "He sent it with me."

"So why didn't he come himself and meet me?" Clint asked.

"He can't," she said. "He fears for his safety."

"What's the message?"

She crossed her legs, which made her skirt ride up a bit, exposing her boot. No skin, though.

" 'Get out while you can.' "

Clint waited, then said, "That's it?"

"That's it," she said.

"And when are you going to see him again?"

"I don't know," she said. "And really, it's none of your affair. This is government business."

"I see."

She put the brandy snifter down on the tray she'd gotten it from and stood up.

"I have to go."

"So soon?" he asked.

"Why?" she replied. "Did you have something special in mind?"

"The same thing I've had in mind since the first time I saw you," he said. "Same thing we both had on our minds last night."

She sucked her lower lip in between her teeth and said, "Ooh, that's tempting, but I have some errands I have to run today."

"Official business?"

"Exactly."

"Well, why don't you come back later?" he asked. "We can have dinner downstairs, and then come back up here."

Now she bit her lip.

"That's very tempting, but I can't make any promises right now."

"That's okay," he said. "I'll be here."

"Like you were here before?"

"I'm here now," he pointed out.

She approached him and put her arms around his neck. He encircled her waist and pulled her to him. They kissed for a long time, and when they parted she was breathless.

"Oh, all right," she said. "You convinced me. I'll come back later for . . . dinner."

"Dinner and . . ."

"Yes," she said, "dinner and . . ."

He released her and she walked to the door. She knew he was watching her swaying hips.

"Are you going to do it?" she asked, without turning to face him.

"Do what?"

"What Ted wants you to do."

"Oh, that," he said. "I don't know. He might just be trying to keep me out of trouble."

"I suspect he is."

"Well, maybe I want to stay and help him."

She turned to face him squarely.

"That wouldn't be such a good idea."

"Well, I'll think about it," he said. "Maybe in the morning . . ."

"We'll talk about it when I come back later," she said.

"I'll be waiting."

She smiled, blew him a kiss and went out the door in a flurry of long dark hair and skirts.

Clint went to the front window to see if anyone was meeting her on the street. When he didn't see her, he assumed she had remained on the hotel side of the street, or had caught a cab in front.

As messages went, that really wasn't much of one. Whoever had thought it up didn't have much of an imagination. He didn't believe for a minute it had come from Ted Singleton. But it had come from somebody who definitely wanted him out of Sacramento—somebody Amanda Tate knew.

He turned back to the room, which was filled with the scent of Amanda's perfume. At the moment he didn't know good guys from bad guys. Amanda was *supposed* to be good, but there was no way of knowing yet. And Victor Barrett was a known crime boss, but he was helping—or claimed he would help.

It would all come down to Ted Singleton. He was the only one who knew all the players, and what side they were on. Clint had to find him in order to find the answers. Singleton had sent for him, so he must have still felt the bond of friendship, must have felt that Clint would be able to help him.

Clint had no intention of leaving Sacramento until he, too, knew all the players, knew where they stood and knew what had happened to his friend.

And most of all, knew what the hell everybody was chasing!

THIRTEEN

Ben Avery was waiting for Amanda Tate in a cab in front of the hotel. When she came out, the driver stepped out to open the door and assist her in.

"Well?" Avery asked.

"I don't think he believed me," she said, sitting across from him. "I'll have to go back later this evening to reinforce it."

"Maybe I should just have some of the boys take care of him."

"I don't think that would be a good idea, Ben."

"Why not?"

"Because he's the Gunsmith," she said, "and you'd end up with some dead boys. Let me handle him."

"That's what you said about Singleton."

"And I was handling it until you sent some boys in, remember?"

He grumbled.

"Just let me do it my way," she said.

"As long as you don't have to sleep with him to do it," Avery said.

Amanda remained silent. Sex with Ben Avery was a pleasant diversion. Sex with Clint Adams had been excit-

ing and new. She had every intention of going back for
more.

Jerry Ames and Salvatore Romanowski—called Roman by
everyone who worked for Victor Barrett—entered the tavern and walked over to Barrett's table.

"Sit down, boys," Barrett said. "I've got some work for
you to do."

"What kinda work, Mr. Barrett?" Ames asked.

"Somethin' that'll give your backs a rest for a while,"
Barrett said.

"Off the docks?" Roman asked. At twenty-three he'd
been working for Barrett for two years, ever since he'd gotten off a boat from Europe, and he hadn't been off the
docks in all that time. Even the rooming house he lived in
was on the docks—or almost.

"Yes, Roman, off the docks," Barrett said, "Jerry, you're
going to be responsible for Roman."

Ames was forty-four and had been a dockworker all his
life. In fact, he was exactly the kind of man Victor Barrett
had not wanted to become. But he was the kind of man
Barrett knew he could count on.

"Now listen up," Barrett said.

"Can we get a drink first?" Ames asked.

"No," Barrett said, "you can have a drink after—just
one. Now open your ears and shut your mouths . . ."

FOURTEEN

Clint did stay in his hotel this time, mainly because he couldn't think of anything better to do with his time. He could have gone to talk to the law, but what if Ted Singleton was involved in something that was illegal? Going to the law would just get him in trouble. Better to sit tight for now and see what Victor Barrett could come up with. Or see what he could pry out of Amanda Tate.

The hotel had its own bar, next to the dining room, so he decided to go down there and kill some time nursing a beer or two.

The difference between the hotel bar and the tavern owned by Victor Barrett was so great that night and day could not explain it. The wood was mahogany and there was a lot of crystal. In fact, they were roughly the same type of furnishings that were in his suite.

He went up to the bar and a clean-shaven, neatly dressed bartender smiled at him and asked, "What can I get for you, sir?"

"A beer."

The bartender brought him a beautiful amber beer with a nice healthy head on it, in a clear, clean mug. Clint picked it up, took several swallows and found it wonderfully cold and refreshing.

"Looks like you're really enjoying that," the bartender said.

"You don't know the half of it," Clint said. "Much obliged."

"Don't mention it. First time in Sacramento?" the man asked.

"First time in a while," Clint said. "First time in this hotel, though."

"Stayin' with us long?"

"I don't know yet," Clint said. "It depends on a few things."

"'Scuse me," the bartender said, and went to take care of someone else.

Clint decided to leave the bar before the man came back and wanted to talk some more. The bar was about three quarters full, but he was still able to find himself an empty table near the back of the room. The clientele here looked like mostly hotel guests and local businessmen. The only thing the place had in common with the Docksider was that there were no guns in sight.

Clint was just thinking about getting another beer when a man wearing a bowler hat and a stern look entered the bar. He didn't know why, but Clint immediately knew the man was looking for him.

And he knew he was a policeman.

Victor Barrett was removing his trousers when there was a knock on the door.

"Ignore it," the woman on the bed said.

Barrett looked at her. He would have liked to ignore the knock. The woman was blond, naked, extremely well endowed. Barrett liked women in all shapes and sizes, and he had three he literally rotated in and out of his bed. Maxine was the woman he wanted when he felt like getting lost on acres of flesh. She had giant, pear-shaped breasts with large pink nipples; big, fleshy buttocks and thighs. She was in her late twenties, and he knew in a matter of years she'd be considered fat. Right now, though, she was perfect for him—at least on this particular night.

"I can't he told her."

"If you answer that door, you're gonna have to leave," she said, "and then you'll miss out on this." She tossed the sheet away from her so that she was completely naked. She spread her legs, dropped her hand down between her thighs, said, "And this," and touched herself.

"Bitch," Barrett said, but he went to the door.

"Clint Adams?" the man asked.

Clint looked up at him. He was holding a bowler hat in his hand, and Clint would have bet the farm—if he owned one—that the man had a small gun secreted there.

"That's right."

"My name is Inspector Charles Callahan," the man said. "I'd like to talk to you, if I may."

"What's this about, Inspector?"

"Do you know a woman named Julie Silver?"

Clint frowned.

"Can't say I do," he answered, "unless . . ."

"Unless what?"

"Why don't you tell me why you're asking," Clint said, "and then I'll tell you unless what?"

"Fine," Callahan said. "We found a young woman tonight. She's dead, and she had your name and the name of this hotel written on a piece of paper on her person. Is that good enough for you?"

"Sit down, Inspector," Clint said. "Let's talk."

FIFTEEN

"I met a girl named Julie yesterday," Clint told the inspector.

"Julie Silver?"

"I never found out her last name."

"What did she want?"

"Well," Clint said, deciding that—in this case—honesty was the best policy, "I'm not sure. She pointed a gun at me and asked me where it was."

"Where what was?"

"That was it," Clint said. "She wanted to know where 'it' was, did I know where 'it' was."

"And?"

"I told her I didn't."

"And do you, in fact, know what this mysterious 'it' is?"

"No, sir, not at all."

"Mr. Adams, I know your name, and your reputation," Callahan said. "Why are you in Sacramento?"

"I'm here to see a friend."

"Does this friend have a name?"

"Ted Singleton."

"Singleton?"

Clint studied the man's face for any sign of recognition.

"Do you know him?" he asked.

"I never heard of him," Callahan said. "Should I have?"

"I don't know," Clint said. "He's an ex-lawman, wore a badge for almost thirty years. I lost track of him about five or six years back, then I heard from him and he asked me to meet him here."

"In Sacramento?"

"In Sacramento," Clint said, "in this hotel."

"And that meeting was supposed to take place yesterday?"

"That's what I thought."

"And you're still waiting."

"Yes."

Callahan thought for a moment, then said, "Tell me again about the girl."

Clint did, explaining their meeting and how it went. He held back only that the girl claimed that she and Singleton were partners, working for the government. He also held back the name of the other woman who had stuck a gun in his face.

"And she never told you what she was looking for?" Callahan asked again.

"She seemed to think I should already know," Clint explained. "She was frustrated when I didn't."

Callahan sat there a few moments, probably trying to think of more questions.

"Can I get you a drink?" Clint asked.

Callahan looked at him, as if reminded that he was still there.

"I think I'll have a beer," the policeman finally said.

"I'll get it for you."

Clint went to the bar, got two fresh beers and brought them back to the table.

"Thanks," Callahan said.

"Can you tell me how she was killed?" Clint asked.

"She was shot," Callahan said. "Twice. Both times in the chest, at close range."

"Where was she found?"

"In an alley downtown."

"You're welcome to check my gun, Inspector—"

"I'm not saying I suspect you, Mr. Adams," Callahan said. "I'm just trying to figure out the girl's actions. I'm trying to come up with my next question. If you don't know her, and don't know what she was looking for . . . and you haven't seen your friend since you arrived?"

"That's right."

Suddenly, Callahan seemed to remember something. He took a piece of paper from his pocket and handed it across to Clint.

"Recognize that handwriting?"

Clint looked at the paper. It had his name and the name of the hotel on it, just like the inspector had first said. Clint studied it for a moment, then handed it back. He had been right earlier. He couldn't have told the lawman whether or not that was Singleton's writing. He just didn't know.

"I can't," he said. "Sorry."

Callahan drank down half his beer and abruptly stood up.

"Will you be here much longer, sir?" he asked. "And by that I mean staying at this hotel?"

"I'm going to try to find my friend, Inspector," Clint said. "I'll be here until I do, or until I get a lead on where he might be."

"Do me a favor," Callahan said, "and check in with me before you leave our city."

"I can do that, Inspector."

"Thank you," the man said. "And thanks for the drink."

As the policeman left, Clint could think of only one word to describe the man—befuddled.

He knew how he felt.

SIXTEEN

Victor Barrett stepped out into the hall to talk to Jerry and Roman. He'd pulled his trousers back on over his erection.

"Have you got something for me already?" he asked.

Roman had spotted the woman on the bed when his boss opened the door, and now he craned his neck to try to get another look. Jerry slapped his arm to make him stop.

"Boss, we heard Callahan was goin' to the Marsh House Hotel to see Clint Adams."

"Why would the inspector want to see Adams?" Barrett asked.

"Well, they found a dead girl," Jerry said. "The word we got is that she knew Adams—at least, she had his name on her."

"What girl?"

"We don't know," Jerry said. "Some young girl."

"Adams said something about a girl pointing a gun at him," Barrett recalled.

"Maybe he found 'er and killed 'er" Roman said.

"Don't be stupid," Barrett said. "He wouldn't have any reason to do that."

"What do we do, Boss?" Jerry asked.

"Keep tryin' to find out what you can about Ted Singleton," Barrett said. "And have someone watch Adams at his hotel. I want to know where he goes."

"Okay," Jerry said.

"Jerry," Barrett said, grabbing the older man's arm, "pick somebody who won't be seen, all right?"

"I know just the guy, Boss."

"Okay."

Barrett only had to look at Roman to know what he was thinking.

"Okay, kid, take a quick look." He opened the door to his room wide. Maxine was still naked on the bed.

"Give the kid a thriller, Maxine."

At first she looked annoyed, but then a slow smile played across her face and she posed. She gave him a good look at her breasts, getting to her knees and holding them in her hands, and then flopped onto her back and opened her legs to give him a gander at—

"Okay, Boss," Roman said, his face coloring, "we gotta go."

Jerry looked at Barrett, shook his head and said, "She scared him."

"Jesus, Jerry," Barrett said, "get that kid to a whorehouse."

"Yeah, Boss," Jerry said. "After we're done."

"You don't want to take a look, Jerry?" Barrett asked him.

"Naw, Boss," Jerry said. "I seen plenty of naked women before."

"Stay in touch," Barrett said. "You need any money? Dope? Anything else to trade in?"

"I got what I need, Boss," Jerry said. "I'll let ya know if I need more."

"You're a good man, Jer."

"Thanks, Boss."

Barrett thought his men could use a stroking of their egos from time to time. In point of fact Jerry was a good man, and Barrett didn't have many of them working for him these days. It was almost time for him to go on a hiring spree. Maybe it was time for him to spend a little more money and stop hiring men right off the boats.

He went into his apartment and closed the door behind him.

"It's about time," Maxine said. "This gal is in need of a little attention."

"And you're gonna get it, too," he said, finally removing his trousers.

Her eyes widened as his rigid penis came into view, and she said, "Come to Mama!"

SEVENTEEN

After the inspector left, Clint nursed his second beer, thinking about Singleton and the poor girl, Julie. He'd spent all of fifteen minutes with her, but her death angered him. He needed somebody to blame, which meant he had to find Ted, or even Amanda. One of them had to know something about the girl who thought she was Singleton's partner. Or maybe he should just go to Barrett. He was someone who, if he didn't know anything about her murder, could probably find out.

Guiltily—because the young girl was dead and would never have another meal—he suddenly found himself ravenously hungry. Maybe that was just a result of hearing about a violent death. He was alive, so he had to eat. It was only natural.

He finished his beer and walked out into the lobby to cross over to the dining-room side. Because he was preoccupied with both the girl's death and with eating, he didn't notice the man by the front door, watching him.

Inspector Charles Callahan entered the office of his superior, Captain O'Neal, knowing he did not have what the man wanted to hear. Callahan was a young inspector, who had been promoted over the protestations of O'Neal, who had put up his own man for the position, a fellow Irishman. Callahan knew that O'Neal would have liked nothing better than for him to fail, so he had to be careful.

"What have you got for me on this dead girl, Inspector?"

"Not a lot, sir. I—"

"What do you mean, not a lot?" O'Neal demanded. "Didn't the dead girl have a man's name in her pocket when she died?"

"Well, yes sir, but—"

"Did you question this man?"

"I did."

"And?"

"He met the girl yesterday, spoke with her for twenty minutes and never saw her again."

"So he says."

"Yes—"

"And you believe him?"

"Yessir, I do."

"Why?"

"Well sir, it was Clint Adams, and he has a certain rep—"

"I know his reputation, Inspector," O'Neal said. "He's a killer, a gunman."

"That's not exactly true, Captain—"

"Why didn't you haul him in here?"

"Well, sir, there's no evidence—"

"Bring him in and we'll find some evidence." O'Neal pounded his desk with his fist. "Do I have to teach you proper police work, son?"

Here was where Callahan knew he had to stand up for himself, or be rolled over by his superior.

"Sir, with all respect, this is my case and I'm not ready to bring anybody in yet."

O'Neal's face was suffused with blood, until Callahan thought the man's head would burst.

"You little piss—" the man started, but then seemed to think better of it. He sat back in his chair, took some breaths, and the redness began to fade from his face. "All right, Inspector. It's your case. You do what you think is best."

"Thank you, sir."

"That'll be all."

"Yes, sir."

Callahan stood up and left the captain's office. He knew what the man was thinking. He'd let Callahan go ahead and do things his way, hoping that it would come back to bite him in the ass. That was okay. Callahan intended to watch his ass very carefully.

O'Neal sat back in his chair and clasped his hands together, resting then on his bloated belly. Callahan was playing right into his hand, and before long his fellow Irishman, Sean O'Casey, would be taking over young Callahan's job. He needed O'Casey to be in place, so that the monthly envelopes from Vincent Barrett did not stop coming. Callahan was honest to a fault, and would never cooperate in the collection of the envelopes.

Once Callahan muffed this homicide case, or got his head handed to him by the killer, he'd be back in uniform walking a beat. A man with a reputation like Clint Adams would eat young Charlie Callahan for breakfast, lunch and dinner.

And Bill O'Neal couldn't wait.

Callahan went back to his own office, a small room barely larger than a closet, and found his friend, Lieutenant Powell.

"How'd it go, Charlie?" Powell asked.

"Not good," Callahan said. "I don't see how much longer I can go before he finally gets me, Sam."

"Well, if he wants to get you, he probably will," Powell said, "unless."

"Unless what?"

"Unless you make it impossible."

"And how do I do that?"

Powell stood up and walked around the desk, put his hand on his friend's shoulder.

"Solve the girl's murder."

"I'm trying."

"Any suspect?"

"Well . . . not a suspect, but she had his name on a piece of paper in her pocket. O'Neal wants me to bring him in."

"Then why don't you?"

"I talked with him, Sam," Callahan said. "I believe him when he says he barely knew the girl."

"Who is this guy?"

"Clint Adams."

"The Gunsmith?"

"That's right."

"Well, Charlie," Powell said, "if he didn't do it, then get him to help you find out who did."

"Why would he help me?"

"Tell him your boss wants you to arrest him," Powell suggested, "and unless you locate the real killer, that's what you're gonna have to do."

"But—"

"But nothin'," Powell said. "You want to go back to wearing a uniform?"

"No."

"Then press Adams into service," Powell said. "He's got a rep, and I heard he's solved a murder or two in his time."

"Really?"

"And if nothin' else, you can use him to scare people

into talkin' to you," Powell added. "Do it, Charlie. Your career depends on it."

After his friend left, Callahan sat behind his own desk, looked around his tiny office and asked himself aloud, "This is a career?"

EIGHTEEN

Clint spent the rest of the night in his room alone, first cleaning his guns, then reading a Mark Twain novel. He'd met Twain briefly some years ago and had become a fan of his work.

He'd hoped to hear from Barrett sometime that night, but by the time he finally closed the Twain book to turn in, there was no word. Maybe he'd hear something in the morning.

He blocked the door with a chair, set the room's pitcher and basin on the windows as a warning system, then went to sleep. He didn't want to wake up to any more guns being stuck in his face, especially not by women.

He had breakfast in the hotel dining room the next morning, and was surprised when Inspector Charles Callahan reappeared. He'd been hoping for Barrett, or an emissary.

The policeman located him in the crowded dining room and came over to his table.

"Good morning, Inspector."

"Mr. Adams."

"Care to join me?"

"I had breakfast, thanks," Callahan said. "but I will join you for a cup of coffee."

"Please," Clint said.

There was already a second cup on the table. Clint turned it right side up and poured the inspector a full cup.

"Thank you."

"Did you think of some more questions you didn't ask last night?" Clint asked.

"No, not exactly," Callahan said.

"What brings you out so early then?"

Callahan sipped his coffee and set the cup down. Clint could see the younger man was wrestling with something.

"You see, I have this captain," Callahan said, finally. "His name's O'Neal?"

"Okay."

"He wants me to arrest you."

"For what?"

"Suspicion of murder."

"Because of the girl having my name in her pocket?" Clint asked. "That's pretty flimsy grounds to arrest me, Inspector, don't you think?"

"As a matter of fact, I do," Callahan said. "That's why I'm not going to do it."

"Won't that get you in trouble with your captain?" Clint asked.

"Oh, yeah," Callahan said, "and he's just looking for an excuse to get rid of me."

"So you came here to tell me you're not going to arrest me?"

"Not exactly," Callahan said. "I actually came here to ask you for your help."

"To do what?"

"To prove to my captain that you didn't kill Julie Silver."

Clint studied the young man while finishing the last bite of his steak and eggs.

"There's only one way to do that," he said, after swallowing.

"And that is?"

"To find out who did kill her."

"Well," Callahan said, "that's my job . . . but I thought you might want to help."

"Let me get this straight," Clint said. "I either help or get arrested for murder?"

"That's not the way I would have put it," the young inspector said, "but that's the way it might actually come out. So . . . yes."

NINETEEN

"I'm not a detective."

"I've heard that your reputation has many facets," Callahan said.

"Meaning?"

"Meaning I heard that you have solved a murder or two in your time."

Clint sat back in his chair and stared at the young man.

"I'm going to help you," he said, finally.

"Well . . . good. Thanks."

"But I want the truth."

"About what?"

"Who put you up to this?"

"I'm sorry . . . up to what?"

"Somebody told you to pressure me into helping you," Clint said. "You didn't think this up on your own."

"I don't—"

"Was it Ted Singleton?"

"I told you last night, I don't know who that is."

"Yes, and I told you last night I didn't know the dead girl for anything but twenty minutes. Yet here you are, back again, asking me to help find out who killed her, when she's a perfect stranger to me."

"Mr. Adams, I—"

"What about Barrett? Was it Barrett?"

"Barrett?"

Clint immediately wished he could bite his tongue off.

"Do you mean Victor Barrett?" Callahan asked. "You know Victor Barrett?"

"We're acquainted."

"When . . . how . . . I thought you said you haven't been to Sacramento for a long time."

"I did say that."

"Then how do you know Barrett?"

"I heard of him," Clint said, "and thought he might be able to help me find my friend Ted."

"Well, that explains it," Callahan said.

"Explains what?"

"Why there is a Barrett man watching the hotel. He's watching you."

"There's a man watching me?"

"He's very good at it," Callahan said. "He's blending in quite well."

"Is he in the lobby?"

Callahan shook his head.

"Across the street."

Clint was annoyed that someone was watching him and he hadn't caught him. Barrett must have picked him because he was good at watching and following someone in the city. Out on the trail Clint would have seen him right away.

"All right, Inspector," Clint said, "what do you want me to do?"

"Well, Mr. Adams—"

Clint held up his hand and said, "Call me Clint. What do you like, Charles or Charlie?"

"I like Inspector."

"I figured, since it must be a fairly new rank for you."

"Well . . . yeah, a month."

"Well, I like Charlie," Clint said. "That's what I'm going to call you."

"Fine."

"What do you want from me, Charlie?"

"I want you to come with me to talk to the people in the neighborhood where Julie Silver was found."

"And?"

"Talk to them."

"You want me to scare them, don't you?" Clint asked. "With my big bad reputation."

"Well . . ."

"Don't you have big, scary policeman in your department?"

"Big maybe," Callahan said, "but none as scary as you will be."

"Charlie," Clint said, "you're wearing a gun, right? Under you arm?"

"Yes."

"A thirty-two, I'll bet."

"How did you know?"

"It fits there comfortably," Clint said. "You're going to have to realize that you don't wear a gun because it's comfortable, you wear it because you want it to save your life."

"What are you suggesting?"

"That you wear a bigger gun."

"I don't have a bigger gun."

"Well, let me tell you this," Clint said. "I'm not going out on the street with you unless I know you can back me up in a fight."

"I can handle myself."

"A bigger gun, Charlie," Clint said. "Either we get you a bigger gun, or I'm not helping."

Callahan stared at Clint just long enough to determine that he was serious, then said, "Fine, I'll carry a bigger gun."

TWENTY

"I didn't mean you were going to have to buy me a gun," Charlie Callahan complained. "I have money."

"I'm not going to buy it for you," Clint said, as they entered the gun shop. "I'm going to pick it out for you."

"Oh."

The shop was as fully equipped as any Clint had seen. He could have spent all day there, talking with the proprietor, who was himself a gunsmith and had been one for thirty years, but they didn't have time. So he picked out a good-looking Peacemaker and then shed a tear as he had the owner cut it down to fit Callahan's shoulder holster.

"It's a forty-five," Clint said, "and even with the cut-down barrel it'll have more kick than that thirty-two you carry."

He turned to the owner.

"Do you have somewhere we can test it?"

"Out back," the man said, then shook his head. "Imagine that, the Gunsmith himself in my shop."

Clint took Callahan outside, behind the building, where the owner had a firing range. Paper targets were affixed to thick bales of hay, so the bullets would not pass through.

"Okay," Clint said, "go ahead."

"How many shots?" Callahan asked.

"All six. I want to see what you can do."

Callahan fired six shots. They all hit the bales of hay. Only three of the six struck the paper target. None hit the bull's-eye. In fact, none were even near it.

"It's cut down," Callahan complained. "Of course I can't hit anything. You ruined it."

"Reload," Clint said.

As Callahan obeyed, the owner of the shop came out to watch. When the gun was reloaded, Callahan cocked the hammer.

"No," Clint said, "not you. Me."

He stepped forward and took the gun. Callahan stepped away. Clint turned toward the target and fired six quick shots. All six struck the paper target. Five of them encircled the bull's-eye, and the sixth was dead center.

"It's perfect."

"You only got one bull's-eye," Callahan said, weakly.

The owner started to laugh.

"Son," he said, "he put every shot right where he wanted it. That's a good gun."

Shaking his head, he went back inside.

Clint ejected the spent shells, reloaded the weapon and gave it to Callahan.

"I'll try again," the younger man said.

"Never mind."

"Why?"

"Because if we get into trouble, you won't be shooting at a paper target," Clint said. "You hit the hay bales, that's good enough for me. You'd hit a man."

"But—"

"You want to investigate your murder, don't you?" Clint asked.

"Well, yes—"

"Then let's go and do some police work."

●   ●   ●

"This is where she was found?" Clint asked.

"Right here."

Clint looked down the dirty alley where Julie Silver's body had been found, then looked down the street.

"How far from the docks are we?"

"About two blocks."

"What the hell was she doing down here?"

"That's what we need to find out," Callahan said.

Clint figured if they were two blocks from the docks, they were two blocks from the Docksider Tavern. Could there be a connection?

He walked into the alley and looked around.

"Where was she found?"

"Against that wall." Callahan entered the alley and pointed.

Clint walked to the wall and saw blood on the ground, lots of it.

"She bled a lot."

"The coroner said she bled to death."

"Poor kid," Clint said. "Probably laid here—what, all night?"

"That's what we think," Callahan said. "Shot the night before last, found yesterday morning."

"By who?"

"A drunk looking for a place to piss."

Clint slapped his hand against the side of the brick building.

"What's this place?"

"Warehouse."

"Abandoned? Empty?"

"No," Callahan said. "In use."

"You question the owner?"

"I tried," Callahan said. "He wouldn't talk to me. Had a few . . . men with him."

"You talked to him alone?"

"Yes."

"That took guts."

"I didn't have a choice," Callahan said. "My boss won't give me any men."

"He really does want you to fail, doesn't he?"

"Yes."

"What'd you do to him?"

"He had someone else in mind for this promotion," Callahan said. "I got it, and I'm trying to hold onto it."

"He doesn't care anything about the girl, does he?" Clint asked.

"No," the inspector said. "All he cares about is me failing. If I don't solve this case, I don't keep my promotion."

"Well," Clint said, "let's see what we can do about that."

"How?"

"First," Clint said, slapping the side of the building again, "let's go and talk to the owner of this warehouse."

TWENTY-ONE

As Clint and Callahan walked around to the front of the warehouse, Clint said, "Looks like our tail is still there."

"Ah, you've spotted him," the inspector said. "Do you want to confront him?"

"I don't think we need to," Clint said. "Looks like Barrett is just keeping an eye on me—or you."

"Me? Why me?"

"Who knows?"

"No," Callahan said, shaking his head, "he's watching you. He was already at the hotel this morning when I got there."

"Either way," Clint said, "he's not doing any harm just watching."

When they got to the front, Clint pounded on the door first with the flat of his hand, and then with his fist, until someone unlocked and opened it.

A man with a face that had encountered many fists in its time asked, "Whataya want?"

Callahan showed the man his badge.

"You again?" the man asked.

"Yes, me again," Callahan said. "My friend and I would like to talk to your boss."

"My boss?"

"The owner of the warehouse?" Clint said. "Is he around?"

"He don't come around here," the man said. "I run the warehouse."

"Is that a fact?" Clint asked. "Were you running it two nights ago?"

"I'm here every night."

"Well," Callahan said, "we're only interested in two nights ago."

"Can we come inside and talk?" Clint asked.

"Nobody comes inside," the man said.

"Then step out here so we can talk," Clint said.

"I don't wanna talk," the man said, and started to close the door. Clint stopped him.

"It's going to be one or the other, friend," he said. "Either we come in, or you step out."

Clint could feel Callahan tense next to him, but he could tell from looking in the man's eyes that there wasn't going to be a problem.

The man looked at Clint, then at Callahan, then back at Clint, and slowly stepped outside and closed the door behind him. He stepped down when he came out, but still towered over both the other men. Callahan couldn't figure out how Clint had intimidated him into stepping outside. They still had not mentioned Clint's name.

"Whataya want?"

"What's your name?"

"Mervin."

"Really?" Callahan asked.

"Yeah." Mervin looked at Callahan. "What about it?"

"Nothing," Callahan said.

"Mervin, a girl was found dead in the alley next to this building."

"I heard." Mervin looked at Callahan. "He told me yesterday."

.

"Well, she was shot twice, probably at night. We want to know if you heard anything."

"I didn't hear nothin'."

"If you did, would you tell us?"

"Probably not."

Clint appreciated the man's honesty.

"Was anyone here with you the other night?"

"Naw," he said. "I was alone, goin' over the books for the boss."

"You do the books?" Callahan asked.

"Yeah." Mervin stuck his anvil of a jaw out pugnaciously. "What, I don't look smart enough?"

"You look plenty smart," Clint said, and gave Callahan a warning look.

"Look," Mervin said, "I'm sorry as hell some girl got killed, but I didn't hear nothin' and I had nothin' to do with it."

"We never said you did," Clint said. "We're just looking for information."

"Well, I got none."

Clint figured they had gotten all they were going to get out of Mervin.

"Okay," Clint said. "Thanks."

They turned to leave, and Mervin opened the door to go back inside.

"Oh, one more thing," Clint said.

"What?"

"Your boss," Clint said. "Who is he? Who owns this warehouse?"

Mervin hesitated, then with a shrug said, "No harm in sayin'. It's owned by Victor Barrett."

TWENTY-TWO

Clint and Callahan got away from the docks and stopped at the first saloon they came to.

"I notice you drink on duty," Clint said, as they took beers to a table.

"I don't know how much longer I'll be on duty, so it probably doesn't matter."

They sat down, looked around. There were only three other men in the place, and one was the bartender. And maybe they were far enough from the docks to be out of Victor Barrett's earshot—except for the man outside, who had followed them.

"So Barrett owns the warehouse," Callahan said. "Could be a coincidence."

"I hate coincidences," Clint said.

"But if you hadn't gone and sought him out," Callahan reminded him, "you never would have heard of him until now. And it wouldn't seem to be a coincidence."

"Whatever the reason was that I went looking for him, now it's a coincidence. And I don't like it."

"But you said he agreed to help you," Callahan argued. "Why would he do that if he had anything to do with the girl's death?"

"To cover for himself."

"So how do we uncover what he's covering?"

"Easy," Clint said. "We go and talk to him again."

"Again?"

"Well, again for me," Clint said. "First time for you."

"There's something you should know about Barrett," Callahan said.

"What? That he's got policemen on his payroll?" Clint asked.

"H-how could you know that?"

"A man like Victor Barrett doesn't get where he is without buying some law, kid," Clint said. "I wouldn't be surprised if he's got your captain in his pocket. Maybe a lieutenant or two."

"My captain wouldn't surprise me," Callahan said.

"You got a lieutenant you're friends with?"

"Yes."

"Can he help us?"

"If he wants to risk his job."

"Well," Clint said, "then we won't ask unless we have to."

"So we're going to see Barrett?"

"Yes."

"I think we'll need an appointment."

"I saw him before without one," Clint said, "but I have an idea."

"What?"

"Just follow my lead." He looked around. "Does this place have a back door?"

Randy Teller watched the front of the saloon closely. When given a job, he usually gave it all his concentration. He was very good at tailing people, keeping them in sight while remaining unseen himself. However, he had one flaw. He sometimes concentrated so much on what was in front of him that he lost sight of what was around him. That was why he was shocked when Clint Adams came up on his left side, and Charlie Callahan moved up on his right.

"Do you know this young fellow, Inspector?" Clint asked.

"Yeah, as a matter of fact I do," Callahan said. "How you doin', Randy?"

"Inspector."

"We need your help, Randy," Callahan said.

"With what?" Randy asked. "I'm just . . . I ain't doin' nothin'."

"We know," Clint said, "that's why we know you have time to help us."

"With what?" he asked, again.

"We want to see your boss," Clint said.

"My boss?"

"Victor Barrett," Callahan said, "remember?"

"Aw, look—"

"It's okay," Clint said, "I saw him yesterday. He and I are good friends now. All you have to do is take us to him."

"So we don't get shot going in," Callahan said. "Some of your friends like to shoot at policemen."

"Look, fellas—"

"You don't have a choice," Clint said, putting his hand on the man's shoulder.

"Let's just go now and get it over with," Callahan said, placing his hand on the man's other shoulder. "If we do it quick, it won't be so painful."

Randy closed his eyes. He was going to be in so much trouble!

TWENTY-THREE

Clint realized how lucky he'd been the day before when he had just blindly walked into the Docksider Tavern.

He had attracted some looks then, but today—walking in with Randy and with a policeman—he got even more.

The first thing he noticed was that Barrett was not at his back table.

They walked up to the bar, and the bartender ignored Clint and Callahan and said, "Randy, what the hell—"

"I didn't have no choice. They wanna see the boss."

"Where is Barrett?" Clint asked.

"We don't serve no law here," the bartender said, glaring at Callahan.

"I wouldn't drink here if it was free," the inspector said. "Where's Barrett?"

"I don't know."

"How would you like me to ask that question again while you're in a cell?"

The bartender winced, then said, "The boss is upstairs, where he lives."

"Get him," Clint said.

"Look, I can't—"

"We're saving your ass by not going up there ourselves," Callahan said. "Now get 'im."

Clint gave Callahan a look. The young man was learning.

The bartender said nothing, just threw down the bar rag he was holding and came out from behind the bar. He went to the back of the room and through a doorway.

"Randy, you can go," Clint said.

"Um—" He seemed unsure about what to do.

"Why don't you just wait outside for us," Callahan suggested, "and then you can follow us some more."

Randy stared at both of them for a few moments, then shrugged and went outside.

After a few minutes the bartender reappeared with an annoyed-looking Victor Barrett behind him.

"Mr. Adams," he said. "I thought we had an agreement that you'd wait to hear from me. Now you're back with a policeman?"

"Actually," Callahan said, "it's the other way around, Mr. Barrett."

"And who are you?"

"I'm Inspector Callahan."

"Ah," Barrett said, smiling. "I've heard about you. What can I do for you, Inspector?"

"You own a warehouse a few blocks from here, just off the docks."

"I own a lot of buildings, Inspector," Barrett said. "Which one are we talking about?"

"The one where a dead girl was found in the alley," Clint said.

"Dead girl," Barrett said. "You mean that homeless young girl who was shot?" He looked at Clint. "Was that the girl you and I were talking about?"

"It was," Clint said, "and she wasn't homeless." Although, for the moment, according to Callahan, she might well have been, since they hadn't been able to find out where she lived.

"But she is dead," Callahan said, "and she was left outside your building."

"As I said, I own a lot of buildings," Barrett said. "I'll bet there have been quite a few bodies found near some of them. After all, it's that kind of area."

"So you don't know a girl name Julie Silver?" Callahan asked.

"Don't know her," Barrett said, "and never did. And Mr. Adams? I'm afraid our little agreement is over."

"That's okay," Clint said. "I pretty much decided I made a mistake coming over here."

"Maybe," Barrett said, "a bigger mistake than you know."

TWENTY-FOUR

"Well," Callahan said, after they'd returned to Clint's hotel, "now you're on the wrong side of Victor Barrett. Congratulations."

"Okay, okay," Clint said, "I already admitted going to him was a mistake. Don't rub it in."

"I just want you to understand this is different than getting some town boss mad at you," Callahan said. "He won't even pick up a gun; he'll just have you killed."

"He's got no reason to have me killed."

"He doesn't need a reason."

"What about you?"

"He could have me killed, too."

"It wouldn't be smart to kill a lawman."

"Maybe he'd make it look like an accident."

"Come on," Clint said, "I'll buy you a beer."

They went into the bar and found it practically empty at that time of the day.

"Two beers," Clint told the bartender.

"Yes, sir."

"Okay," Clint said to Callahan. "Just because the girl was found in an alley next to a building owned by Barrett doesn't mean he had anything to do with killing her."

"Agreed," Callahan said, "but on the other hand, he wasn't very cooperative."

"No, he wasn't."

"And Randy is still tailin' us—you."

"That's okay," Clint said. "We may have some use for Randy again."

The bartender brought their beers and they went to a back table.

"Is it true that the gunmen of the old West always sat with their backs to the wall after Wild Bill Hickok was killed?"

"Let's just say it's smart to sit where you can see the entire room."

"Much like you are now?"

"Exactly."

Callahan moved his shoulders, then adjusted his jacket.

"You'll get used to it," Clint said.

"What?"

"The bigger gun. It's uncomfortable now, but you'll get used to it."

"I don't know," Callahan said. "Maybe I should just wear it on my hip, like you do."

"Have you ever worn a gun and hip holster?"

"Years ago," Callahan said. "I wasn't very good with it."

"Stick to the shoulder rig then," Clint said. "Go back to your smaller gun after I leave town."

"Like you said," Callahan responded, hitching his shoulders again, "I'll get used to it."

They sipped their beer in silence for a few moments, and then Callahan said, "What do we do now? I need to make something happen."

"So do I," Clint said. "I'm still trying to find my friend. I only hope he's alive." Then he decided to tell Callahan something he hadn't told him yet. "Charlie, do you know a woman named Amanda Tate?"

Callahan sat up straight.

"What do you know about Amanda Tate?"

"I met her the same day I met Julie," Clint said.

"Under what circumstances?"

"Much the same."

"You mean . . ?"

"She stuck a gun in my face."

"So she's looking for this . . . whatsit, too?"

"Apparently. Who is she?"

"She runs with a man named Ben Avery."

"And who is Ben Avery?"

"He's what Victor Barrett was a few years ago," Callahan said. "He hopes to compete with Barrett someday soon."

"Do you know where to find Ben Avery?"

"I do," the young inspector said, "but tell me more about you and Amanda first."

"What do you want to know?"

"Did she know the other girl? Julie?"

"I think she may have."

"And your friend?" Callahan asked. "Singleton? Did she know him?"

"She claims she did."

Callahan digested the information for a few moments before speaking again.

"Have you checked hospitals for your friend?" he asked.

"No," Clint said. "Couldn't quite bring myself to do that, yet."

"If he's been involved with Victor Barrett and Ben Avery," Callahan said, "I think it may be time."

TWENTY-FIVE

Ben Avery may have wanted to compete with Victor Barrett, but he didn't want to live on the docks. Instead, according to Callahan, he lived and operated out of a hotel on K Street.

But they didn't want Barrett's man, Randy, following them there.

"You get us a cab out front," Clint told Callahan while they were still in his hotel, "and I'll get rid of Randy."

"Get rid of—" Callahan said. "You're not gonna—"

"No, I'm not going to kill him," Clint said. "You can't believe all the stories you hear, Charlie."

"Sorry," Callahan said, "I didn't mean—"

"Forget it, kid," Clint said. "Come on, get that cab and I'll join you in a minute."

They went out the front door together. Callahan stopped to wave down a cab while Clint crossed the street and approached an apprehensive-looking Randy, who put both his hands up.

"Wait, wait . . ."

"Randy," Clint said, handing him some money, "go into my hotel and wait in the bar."

"Huh?"

"Buy some drinks and wait. We'll be back soon."

"B-but—"

"Look, I'm keeping you out of trouble," Clint said. "I don't want you to follow us, and if you have to tell your boss you lost us, he won't like it. Right?"

"Uh, yeah, r-right." He still looked confused.

"So go into my hotel, have some drinks, and wait. We'll be back."

"Well . . . o-okay," Randy finally said. "I guess that's okay."

"Sure it is. Come on."

Clint walked Randy across the street and into the hotel, then joined Callahan in the cab.

"What'd you do?"

Clint explained.

"That was . . . brilliant."

"I know," Clint said. "Did you tell the driver where we're going?"

"Yep. Drive on, driver!"

The driver snapped his reins and the cab started moving.

When they reached the residential hotel where Ben Avery lived, they had to present themselves to a doorman who looked—and talked—like an ex-fighter.

"State yer business," he said.

"This is my business," Callahan said, showing his badge.

"And him?"

"He's with me."

"I gotta go up and announce ya."

"Then do it," Callahan said. "We'll wait."

The doorman nodded, then went up the stairs to the second floor.

•   •   •

"Get that," Avery told one of his men. There were two in the room, Daly and Gomes, and both were armed. Amanda was there, but she was in the bedroom.

Gomes went to the door and opened it.

"It's the doorman, Boss."

Avery didn't look up from his desk.

"What's he want?"

"He says there are two policemen downstairs to see you."

Avery looked up. "Where are they?"

"In front of the hotel."

"Not inside?"

Gomes asked. "No, out front."

Avery got up and went to his window. He opened it and peered out and down. One man looked like a policeman, one didn't. In fact, one looked like—

"Daly, get Amanda."

"She might not be dressed, Boss."

"I don't care. Get her out here."

"Sure, Boss."

Daly went to the bedroom, let himself in and was greeted by a shriek. Moments later he came out with Amanda, who was trying to tie a robe around herself. One big breast was in full view, pink nipple and all, and she hurriedly buried it.

"What the hell—"

"Shut up and come here," Avery hissed.

She knew that tone. She joined him at the window.

"What?"

"Look down there."

She looked.

"Two men," she said.

"Look again."

She sighed, looked again, then stared hard. "What the—"

"Who is that?"

"I don't know who the bowler hat is," she said, looking at him, "but the other one is Clint Adams."

"The bowler hat is a policeman," he said, closing the window. "Okay, you go in the bedroom, and stay there."

She hurried to do that.

"Daly, tell the doorman to let them up."

"Okay, Boss."

"Gomes," he said, "you stand in that corner and watch them the whole time."

"Should I take out my gun—"

"Not unless I tell you to. Daly, you let them in and then stand in that corner. Same thing. Understand?"

"Yes, sir."

"I don't know what these fellas want," Avery said, "but if I say the word, they're dead. Not before. You got it?"

"We got it, Boss," Daly said, and Gomes nodded.

Avery went around behind his desk and waited to greet his visitors.

TWENTY-SIX

The doorman let them go up and stayed behind. The stairway to the second floor was narrow, and Clint realized that if this was an ambush they were as good as dead. Luckily, they made it to the top of the stairs without incident.

At the top they encountered another man, built along the lines of the doorman.

"You got guns?" He looked pointedly at the gun on Clint's hip, then looked at Callahan, who pulled back his jacket to show his.

"And we're keeping them," Clint said.

The man gave him a hard look, but finally stepped aside to allow them to enter. Clint immediately detected the scent of Amanda's perfume in the air, but she was nowhere in sight.

There was a desk at the far end of the room, and a man seated behind it. Around the room were several pieces of expensive furniture, but there didn't seem to be any rhyme or reason as to how they were situated.

Clint noticed one bodyguard type standing in one corner with his big hands clasped before him, and the man from the stairs moved to another corner. Now they were in position for a crossfire.

As they approached the desk, Clint made sure to bump into Callahan, pushing him farther away from him. The younger man took the hint and moved until they were several feet apart by the time they reached the desk.

"Ben Avery," Callahan said, showing his badge, "I'm Inspector Callahan."

"Inspector," Avery said. "Who's your friend?"

"His name is Clint Adams." Callahan didn't explain any further.

Avery looked at Clint. The man was clean-shaven, young-looking, maybe twenty-six. It was surprising that he was in a position of such power—if, indeed, he wielded any power outside this room.

"I've heard of you," he said. "Your legend precedes you. It's an honor."

Clint just nodded at the compliment and waited for Callahan to speak.

"Mr. Avery, do you know a girl named Julie Silver?" the inspector asked.

"Julie Silver?" Avery stopped to think a moment. Clint knew what he was going to say before he said it, and thought that Ben Avery was possibly the worst liar he'd ever met.

"No, I can't say I do."

"And Amanda Tate?" Clint asked.

"Amanda? Sure, I know Amanda. Why? Is she all right?" he asked.

"As far as I know," Clint said. "But, see, Amanda knew Julie, so I think it would make sense that you knew her, too."

"Knew her?"

"She's dead," Callahan said. "Murdered two nights ago."

Avery looked surprised, and Clint believed that the man had not known that.

"That's . . . terrible."

"Shot twice and left in an alley next to a building owned by Victor Barrett."

"Victor? Well, there's your answer. Why aren't you askin' Victor if he knew her? Or killed her?"

"We did ask him," Callahan said. "He claims not to have known her."

"So why come to me?"

"Amanda," Clint said.

Avery looked at Clint.

"If Amanda knew her, talk to Amanda. That doesn't mean I knew her."

"Amanda was here today," Clint said. "I can smell her perfume."

"You have a real good nose," Avery said. "Yeah, she was here, but now she's not." He turned his attention to the policeman. "Are you here to arrest me?"

"No, sir," Callahan said. "We just wanted to ask you a few questions."

Clint saw Avery look at his two men, and felt them relax. Somehow he'd sent them a message to "stand down." He might have felt he was in danger from Clint and Callahan when they first arrived, but he didn't anymore. And he was lying about Amanda. She was probably in another room.

"Have I answered them?"

"Yes, you have."

"Then I guess we're done here."

Callahan looked at Clint, who nodded slightly.

"All right, then," Callahan said. "Thanks for your time."

"No problem."

"We can find our way out," Clint said.

"It was a pleasure to meet you, Mr. Adams." Avery stood and shook hands with Clint, then clasped his hands in front of him before Callahan could think he was going to do the same.

Clint and Callahan turned and went back down the tight hallway stairs.

TWENTY-SEVEN

When they got outside in front of the building, Callahan said, "I had more questions."

"We found out what we needed to know."

"And what was that?"

"He knew the girl."

"How could you tell that?"

"He was lying."

"And how could you tell that?" Callahan asked, frustrated.

"Because he is very, very bad at it," Clint said.

"What exactly did he lie about?"

"He lied about knowing Julie Silver, and he lied about knowing where Amanda was."

"What about killing the girl?"

"No," Clint said, "he didn't do it, and before you ask me how I knew that—he was surprised that she was dead."

"Yeah," Callahan said, "I thought that, too."

"You just have to learn how to read people Charlie," Clint said.

"Okay," Callahan said, "so if he knows where Amanda is, where is she?"

"My guess is she's still up there."

"So now we watch?"

Clint turned and looked at the doorman, who was eye-
ing them suspiciously.

"So now we find a place to watch from," Clint said,
grabbing Callahan's arm.

When Amanda came out of the bedroom, she was dressed.

"You two," Avery said to his men, "out."

Without a word they left.

"Did you know Julie was dead?" he demanded.

"No, lover," she said, "but I don't mind a bit that she is."

"Damn it, Amanda."

She came up behind him and wrapped her hands around
his chest, leaning her breasts against the back of his neck.

"It was just an infatuation, darling," she told him in his
ear.

"You had her killed, didn't you?" he demanded.

"How could I do that, Ben?" she asked. "Everyone
knows you're the boss."

He lifted her hands off him and stood up, turning to
face her.

"Are you going to hit me now?"

"I should," he said. "I should give you a beatin'."

"If you do that," she said, chuckling, "you know what
will happen. We'll end up in bed, fucking our brains out.
That girl, that Julie, she would never have understood that
kind of passion."

"She might have learned."

"Not that one," Amanda said. "She was a straight arrow."

He stood there, almost pouting. She walked up to him
and took his face in her hands.

"Believe me, Ben," she said, "she wasn't for you."

"You didn't kill her?"

"No."

"Because if I thought you did—"

"But I didn't." She kissed him shortly on the mouth.

"Now, I have to go and run some errands, sugar, but when I come back, Mama wants to fuck. Okay?"

When she kissed him this time, she sucked his tongue into her mouth and slid one hand down between them to feel his hardness through his trousers.

"Oh yes," she said, petting him, "when I come back, you'll forget all about Julie Silver."

TWENTY-EIGHT

Clint and Callahan had barely secured a spot across the street when Amanda came walking out the front of the building. She said something to the doorman, who almost bowed to her, then followed her progress with a hungry look as she walked down the street.

They were lucky she didn't wave down a cab, because at that moment only one went by. They would not have been able to follow.

"Let's go," Clint said.

"Stay on this side of the street, Clint," Callahan told him.

"I know how to follow somebody, Callahan," Clint told him.

"Yeah, but this is the city."

"I've been to cities before," Clint said. "Come on, we don't want to lose her."

"Are we hoping she'll lead us to the killer?" Callahan asked.

"Or to Ted Singleton."

"They might be one and the same," Callahan said.

"I sure hope not."

• • •

Ben Avery watched from his window as Amanda Tate went walking up the street at a brisk pace. Their relationship was confusing to him. The sex was amazing, even though she was almost fifteen years older than he was. And she was an excellent confidante and adviser to him as he tried to build his business into something that would compete with Victor Barrett. But somehow, he felt there was a barrier between them. She'd flown into a rage when she found out he was attracted to Julie Silver, who was closer to his age. He couldn't be sure, but he was afraid that she'd had Julie killed, and if she did, she'd used one of his men to do it. That meant she was undermining his authority and using his men—at least one of them—behind his back.

Avery had been thinking lately that it might be time to break away from Amanda Tate. And if she had, indeed, orchestrated Julie's death, he knew just how he was going to do it.

That was why when he saw Clint Adams and Inspector Callahan follow her up the street, he simply turned and walked to his desk.

Amanda's pace was quick, as if she knew where she was going and was in a hurry to get there. And where she was going was literally only a few blocks away and around a corner and then she was there. A hotel.

"Uh-oh," Callahan said.

"What?"

"A woman going to a hotel in the middle of the day," the policeman said.

"What about it?"

"I don't know what that would mean in Dodge City or Tombstone," Callahan said, "but here it means a woman is meeting a man—a man who is not her husband."

"It wouldn't happen in Dodge City or Tombstone," Clint said, "and Avery is not her husband."

"Her man, then," Callahan said. "She's meeting someone other than her man."

Clint frowned. Obviously, she and Avery had a sexual
relationship, and she had also been to bed with Clint. Now
she was meeting another man? Singleton, or a new player
in the game?

He hoped it was Singleton. At least then he would have
found him.

And he also wished he knew what the damn game was.

Amanda already had a key, because she came to this hotel
fairly often—often enough for the clerk to simply nod to
her. She went up the stairs to the second floor and let herself into a suite there. The man there waiting for her was
already naked, and erect.

"You're not wasting any time today," she said, approv-
ingly.

"It's been a while," he said to her. "Get your clothes
off."

She obeyed.

Clint and Callahan entered the hotel lobby behind
Amanda. She was already gone. They approached the front
desk and the clerk looked at them.

"Gents," he said. "Can I help you?"

Callahan showed him his badge and said, "The lady
who just came in—"

"Room two-fifteen. It's a suite."

Clint and Callahan looked at each other.

"That was easy," Clint said.

"Ain't stickin' my neck out for nobody," the young clerk
said.

"All right, then," Clint said, "next question. Who's she
with?"

"Don't know 'im."

"Does she meet the same man here every time?" Callahan asked.

"Yep, same man."

"How long has this been going on?" Clint asked.

"I dunno," the clerk said. "Months?"

"How many times a week?" Clint asked.

"Couple," he said, "but it's funny, they missed last week, and this is the first time this week."

Clint and Callahan exchanged another glance. Today was Thursday.

"Is there another way out of the hotel?" Callahan asked.

"Not for guests."

"So she and her boyfriend will have to come through the lobby and out the front door?"

"Yep."

"So we wait again?" Callahan asked.

"We wait again," Clint said.

TWENTY-NINE

Amanda lifted her knees to open herself up more for him. He got between her legs, pressed the head of his penis to her moist slit and pushed. His rigid penis slid into her like a hot knife through butter, and she gasped. He began to fuck her then, in long, slow strokes. He said it had been too long and he wanted to take his time, but she didn't have that much time to give him. She urged him on, using her hands and her mouth to excite him more, even using old whore tricks and talking dirty to him, until he was pounding her, snorting like a bull, chasing his release. When it came, he bellowed, jammed himself into her and his whole body shuddered. Then he collapsed on her the way they all did, like because it was all over for them, it was all over for her, too.

Well, in this case it *was* all over. She rolled him off of her, and while he was lying on his back, panting and sweating like a pig, she took the knife out of her purse, a stiletto with a nice thin but strong blade, and stuck it in him once, twice and then a last time, twisting it before she took it out. The sheets quickly began to soak in his blood, and she got off the bed before any of it got on her. He died with a gasp and a rattle, and she threw the bedsheet over him. Immediately, the blood began to soak through that, too.

She'd thought that a good fucking would help her, get her ready to do what she had to do, but it hadn't been very good at all. In fact, she hadn't been fucked good in so long, until the other night with Clint Adams. She didn't know exactly what was going to happen to him, but she knew she was going to get him between her thighs at least one more time. Who knew how long it would be before she came across a real man again?

"I wonder how long they'll be," Callahan said.

"Have you ever met with a woman in a hotel, Charlie?" Clint asked.

"Well, sure . . ."

"Someone else's woman?"

"No."

"They'll be a while," Clint said.

"You've been with somebody's else's woman?"

"Once or twice," Clint said.

"That, uh, don't sound right."

"It isn't," Clint said. "How old are you?"

"I'm, uh, twenty-eight."

"Been with many women?"

"Well, sure . . . I been . . . Well, with a . . . few . . ."

"Don't be embarrassed," Clint said. "You've got plenty of time and a lot to learn."

Upstairs Amanda made sure she had no blood on her. She poured water from a pitcher in a basin, washed herself good, then used a cloth to wash her pussy. It felt good, so she kept washing until she'd finished what the dead man on the bed couldn't. Her body shuddered, her right hand rubbing hard with the cloth, her left hand pinching her own nipples . . .

Afterward she got dressed and looked over again at the bloody lump lying beneath the sheet.

"Too bad," she said to him. "I might've been able to train you to be a good lover."

Now she'd never know, though. However, she was left with Ben Avery, and he was still young enough to learn.

She straightened her clothing, put her knife back in her bag and left the room.

"There she is," Callahan said. "That didn't take real long at all."

"No, it didn't," Clint said, suspiciously.

A cab came by at that moment, and she waved it down and got in.

"We've got to find a cab," Callahan said, stepping out of the doorway they were in.

"No," Clint said, "we have to go upstairs."

"Why?"

"Something's not right."

"Like what?"

"I don't know," Clint said. "If she was just meeting a man here for sex, it should have taken longer. This just feels wrong."

"But we'll lose her."

"I think she's done what she came out to do, Charlie," Clint said. "Besides, I think we know where we can find her. Come on, let's go upstairs and see what she left behind."

THIRTY

Callahan got the key from the clerk at Clint's insistence.

"Why don't we just knock?" he asked.

"Because if I'm right, nobody would answer."

They went up to room 215 and Callahan insisted on knocking first.

"Satisfied?" Clint asked, when no one answered.

Callahan used the key and opened the door. Immediately they saw the blood-soaked sheets on the bed.

"Jesus," Callahan said. "I wonder who it is."

Clint wondered, too. He hoped it wasn't Ted Singleton, but he had a bad feeling that it was.

"Let's have a look," he suggested.

They approached the bed. There was so much blood it was dripping onto the floor.

Clint waited, and when Callahan made no move to pull back the top sheet, he gripped it and gave it a yank.

"Christ," Callahan said, "she gutted him."

The body was naked, and had been stabbed more than once. Clint could see that at least one wound was the result of a stabbing and then twisting of the knife. She hadn't wanted to make any mistakes. She wanted him dead, for sure.

"Christ," Callahan said, again. "This is bad."

They both knew who the man was; they'd seen him earlier. Clint was relieved that the body was not that of Ted Singleton, but Victor Barrett.

Callahan wanted to send for his superior immediately, but Clint made him talk about it.

"If your captain was taking money from Barrett, he's not going to be too happy that we stood out in front of the hotel while Amanda Tate killed him."

"We don't know that she killed him," Callahan said. "He could have been killed after she left, or before she got there."

Clint thought that was naive, but he let it go for the moment.

"That doesn't matter," Clint said. "You'll still find yourself in uniform somewhere. Do you want that?"

"No, of course not, but—"

"But what?"

"We can't just walk away from this," the young inspector said. "For one thing, the desk clerk saw us."

"For the right amount of money, he'll keep quiet," Clint said. "Besides, you showed him your badge, you didn't give him your name."

"He can point me out."

"Stay away from him," Clint said. "Just walk out of the hotel. He won't even notice."

"What about the key?"

"They've got lots of keys."

"Look, Clint, if you want to go—"

"I'm not the one this is going to cause trouble for," Clint said, "you are. Look, I've got an idea."

"What?"

"I'll send for the police. Who will they send here first?"

"Somebody in uniform."

"And then what?"

"Well, normally they'd send word for an inspector," Callahan said, "but once they see who this is, they'll send for someone higher-ranking—a lieutenant or a captain."

"But they'll need an inspector eventually," Clint said. "That could be you."

"How do I make sure—"

"Just go to headquarters and be there when the word comes in," Clint said. "Then you come here like you've never been here before."

"The clerk—"

"I'll take care of the clerk."

Callahan worried his lower lip. He paced around the bed, staring at the body.

"All you have to do is solve this murder, and your trouble will go away, kid," Clint said. "But if they find out you were here—"

"I know, I know!" Callahan snapped. "I'm thinking."

While he was thinking, Clint looked around the room. The first thing he noticed was the smell of blood. Second, Amanda's perfume. She'd been here, all right, and she'd been in bed with the naked man. But had she killed him? Had to be her. Nothing else made sense. What was her motive, though? Just to get Ben Avery's biggest competition out of the way?

"Okay," Callahan said, "okay. I'm going to go. I'll need a half an hour to get back to headquarters."

Clint didn't relish spending half an hour with a dead body, but then, it was his idea. He'd use the time to talk to the clerk, who, since he didn't want to stick his neck out for nobody, might take some convincing.

"Okay," Clint said. "Tell me your friend the lieutenant's name, in case it's him who shows up."

"Powell, Sam Powell."

"Okay," Clint said, "now go."

"Are you sure you're willing to do this?" Callahan asked.

"I'm sure, kid," Clint said. "This all might still help me to find my friend."

"All right," Callahan said. "All right. I'm doing this against my better judgment but . . . all right."

"Go already!"

THIRTY-ONE

Clint stood to the side while the police examined the body on the bed. He'd been told to stay out of the way, which he was only too happy to do . . .

While waiting for the police, he'd had a very earnest talk with the desk clerk, who was appalled that Clint had found a dead body in the hotel.

"I don't stick my neck out for nobody," he said, again.

"I'm not asking you to stick your neck out," Clint said. He put some money on the desk. "I'm just asking you to forget that I was in here asking questions."

The clerk eyed the money.

"What about the other guy with you?"

"Especially forget him."

Clint put some more money on the desk.

"He was a cop," the man said. "Who're you?"

"My name's Clint Adams."

The clerk hesitated, then said, "Really?"

"Yes, really."

The clerk examined him.

"Yeah, you look like him."

"Like who?"

The clerk reached beneath the desk and brought out

three dog-eared, yellow-paged books. On the cover of each was an illustration of a man who looked like Clint. At the top of the book, in large letters, were the words "THE GUNSMITH."

"You're really him?"

"Well . . . ," Clint said, and stopped himself. If he said that he was really him—*that* Gunsmith—it would not be entirely factual.

"Yeah," he said, "I'm really him."

"Can I see your gun?"

Patiently, Clint removed his gun from his holster, unloaded it and handed it to the young man.

"Wow."

Clint took the gun back, loaded it and replaced it in his holster.

"So?" he asked. "We got a deal?"

The man looked at the money on the desk as if he'd forgotten it, then grabbed it.

"Yeah, Mr. Gunsmith, yeah," he said, "we got a deal, only . . ."

"Only what?"

"Will you sign my books?"

He thought about pointing out that he didn't write them, but instead said, "Sure."

Clint was jolted from his thoughts by the arrival of another man, dressed in a suit.

"Hey, Lieutenant," one of the uniformed policeman said.

"Who found him?" the man asked.

The man in uniform inclined his head toward Clint. The lieutenant walked over to him and looked him up and down.

"This ain't Tombstone, partner," he said.

"For some of us," Clint said, "every town, every city is Tombstone."

"So what's your name?"

"Clint Adams."

"Clint . . . Adams?"

"That's right."

"The Gunsmith?"

"Yes."

"You got anything on you that proves that?"

"No," Clint said, then looked down at his gun. "Only this."

The policeman looked unimpressed.

"Lieutenant . . . ?"

"Powell."

"Powell. I'm staying at the Marsh House Hotel. You can check me out with them."

"I won't have to," Powell said. "I know somebody who knows you."

"Here in Sacramento?"

"Yeah." Powell turned, and at that moment Inspector Charles Callahan came through the door.

"Charlie," Powell said, "this fella says he's Clint Adams. Is that him?"

Callahan came over and said, "Yes, sir, that's him. Mr. Adams."

"Inspector," Clint said. "Nice to see you again."

Powell looked from Callahan to Clint and back again, and Clint knew they were in trouble.

"You fellas are funny," he said. He turned to address the room and shouted, "Everybody out."

The men in the room began filing out. One uniformed policeman came over and asked, "What should we do, Lieutenant?"

"Question all the other guests on the floor," Powell said, "see what they saw."

"Yes, sir."

Powell waited for everyone to be gone, then closed the door and turned to face Clint and Callahan.

"What are you two tryin' to pull?"

THIRTY-TWO

"What are you talking about?" Callahan asked.

"Forget it, Charlie," Clint said. "I didn't realize what a lousy liar you were."

"Oh, he always has been," Powell said.

"You can't do anything with him?"

Powell made a face. "He's too damn honest."

"You two want to stop talking about me?" Callahan asked.

"Okay," Powell said, "let's go back to you two. What's going on?"

Clint looked at Callahan, who shrugged and said, "You tell it."

Clint started at the beginning, told Powell everything without leaving anything out.

Powell looked at the body again when Clint had finished.

"Okay," he said.

"Okay, what?" Callahan asked.

"We can keep this from O'Neal—for a while."

"How long's a while?" Clint asked.

"Until we find out who killed Barrett," Powell said. "And the girl . . . and, while we're at it, maybe we can locate your friend."

131

"You'll work with us on this?" Callahan asked.

"No."

"What?"

"That would be sticking my neck out too far," Powell said. "I will cover for you, though, while the two of you work on it."

"Good enough," Clint said.

"You," Powell said, "I've heard of, but I never met before now. Charlie here is a friend of mine."

"I get it," Clint said.

"Get what?" Callahan asked.

Clint looked at him. "He's telling me that if he has to throw somebody to the wolves, it's going to be me."

"Right," Powell said.

"Hey, that's not—"

"It's fine, Charlie," Clint said, cutting him short. "I can live with that. He's right, you're his friend, I'm not."

"But friend or no friend," Powell said to Callahan, "if push comes to shove, you'll go to the wolves before I do."

Clint and Callahan were outside the building when the body was carried out. Lieutenant Powell followed behind the body.

"What's going to happen inside his business now?" Clint asked.

"I don't know," Powell said. "I don't know of anybody who works for him who could take it over."

"That'll leave it for Ben Avery to take over," Callahan said.

"So you think the woman killed Barrett to give Avery that opening?"

"Who knows?" Clint said. "Maybe she did it out of love."

"Not likely," Powell said. "See, I know Amanda. She's been in Sacramento for years. Avery is just her latest conquest."

"Conquest?" Clint asked.

"She goes through men like—well, I don't know like what. Avery's just the next in a long line."

"He's kind of young, isn't he?" Clint asked.

"He's about twenty-eight," Powell said. "Who knows how old she is? Could be thirty-eight, could be forty-eight. She's not talking."

Clint remembered his night with Amanda. However old she was, it had not diminished her performance in bed at all.

The body was dumped unceremoniously into a buckboard and driven away.

"Did he have family?" Clint asked.

"No," Powell said. "I don't know who we'll have to notify that he's dead." He looked at Callahan. "But you'll come up with someone, I'm sure."

"Me?"

"Your case, Inspector," Powell said. "This, and the Julie Silver case. I think they're connected, so you've got both of them."

"How's the captain going to feel about that?" Clint asked.

"Oh, he'll love it," Powell said. "He's just waiting for young Charles here to fail." Powell slapped Callahan on the back. "But I have faith."

Powell had a cab waiting for him, driven by a uniformed policeman.

"Maybe that's the job I should have," Callahan said as his superior rode away.

"What's that?"

"Driving him around."

"Nah," Clint said, "you're better than that, Charlie."

"I guess we'll see about that soon enough."

THIRTY-THREE

Clint and Callahan discussed their next move in a cab going back to Clint's hotel.

"We can go back to Avery's office, grab Amanda and try to prove she killed Barrett," Clint said, "or we can go down to the docks and see what Barrett's men know, if anything."

"I would vote for picking up Amanda," Callahan said, "except I don't think that would help us find your friend—or find out what happened to him."

"Well," Clint said, "with Julie and Barrett both dead, I'm starting to think that Ted's dead, too."

They rode in silence for a while and then Callahan asked, "Just how friendly did you actually get with Amanda anyway?"

"Pretty friendly."

"I guess you're lucky she didn't kill you in your sleep."

Clint looked at Callahan and said, "Who slept?"

When they got to Clint's hotel, they immediately went to the bar. Both needed a beer after the day's events.

"What do we do with the rest of the evening?" Callahan wondered aloud.

"If we go to that Docksider Tavern of Barrett's, it's liable to be filled with his men. They won't take kindly to hearing that he's dead."

"Might even take it out on us."

"Might," Clint said. "I think we better pass that information on tomorrow."

"Agreed."

They clinked their glasses on it. The hotel bar was filling up, and they'd had to stand at the bar with their drinks.

"What about Avery's place?" Callahan asked.

"Do we know if Amanda has her own? Or does she live there with him?"

"My understanding from the lieutenant was that she has her own home—a house, actually."

"Hmm . . . Do we know where it is?"

Callahan smiled, reached in his pocket and took out a slip of paper.

"Just so happens we do."

Clint snatched it from him.

"You stay here," he said, "or go back to headquarters, or go home yourself."

"What are you going to do?"

"I think I'll visit the black widow in her lair," Clint said. "Might get something out of her."

"Or she might get you."

"I'll be careful."

"I can't just do nothing."

"Do some police work, then," Clint said.

"Like what?"

"I don't know," Clint said. "I'm not a policeman. You think of something."

Callahan opened his mouth to say something, but Clint cut him off. "I know. Find out how many men Barrett had, and how many Avery has. We might as well know what we might be going up against."

"I can do that."

"Okay then," Clint said, "let's go."

They finished their beers, went out to the front of the hotel and had the doorman get them each his own cab.

THIRTY-FOUR

Clint had the cab drop him right in front of Amanda's house in a residential section of Sacramento. It was not yet dark, but Clint thought that after killing Victor Barrett, Amanda may have wanted to go home and put her feet up. After all, if she had also killed Julie and Ted Singleton, she'd been a busy gal.

He went up the walk to the front door and knocked. He had to knock a second time before Amanda finally came to the door and opened it.

"Why am I not surprised?" she asked, smiling at him. "How did you find out where I lived?"

"I asked around."

He could tell from the puzzled look on her face that she didn't like that.

"Asked around? Asked who?"

"The police." He said it with a smile.

"Clint," she said, slowly, "I think you better come inside."

She stepped back to allow him to enter, then stuck her head out to have a look before closing the door.

Once they were both inside, she faced him, folding her arms beneath her heavy breasts. She was wearing a simple shirt and skirt, and she was barefoot.

139

"I think you better tell me what the hell you're talking about," she said. "The police told you where I live?"

"That's right."

"Why would they do that?"

"Because I asked them."

"And why would you do that?" she asked. "What's going on?"

"Come on, Amanda," he said. "You know what you did this afternoon."

"Yes, I do know what I did this afternoon," she said. "And, apparently, you think you know, too."

"Well," he said, "after all, I was there."

"There . . . where?"

"Well, for starters," he said, "I was at Avery's place when you were hiding in the other room."

"What makes you think I was hiding in the other room?" she asked.

"I could smell your perfume all over the place."

"That could just mean that I *had* been there," she said, "not that I still was."

"Well then, that part was just a lucky guess."

"And what else do you think you know?"

"Well, I followed you to a hotel where you met with Victor Barrett for some . . . relaxation?"

"So you know I had sex with Victor," she said. "Did you tell Avery?"

"I didn't have a chance to," he said. "You went in, you came out, we went up and discovered poor Victor, all cut up."

"Somebody stabbed him to death?"

"As if you didn't know."

She dropped her hands to her sides. She was breathing hard, and he could not help but watch the swell of her breasts, remembering how they'd felt in his hands—their heft, the smoothness of her skin, the turgid nipples in his mouth . . .

"You think I did it?"

"Let's just say the police are fairly sure."

"Then why are you here and not them?"

"I wanted to give you a chance to explain yourself."

"Look, Clint," she said, "Avery could've killed Barrett out of jealousy."

"We left him at his place when we followed you to that hotel," Clint said. "We never saw him."

"He could've sent someone."

"The only person we saw was you."

"You keep saying 'we'?" she asked. "Who do you mean?"

"Me and a friend."

"A friend who's a policeman?"

"That's right."

"All right," she said, pacing now, "if I killed Victor Barrett, tell me why I did it."

"To put your boy Avery into the top spot in town," Clint said. "To help him take over Victor Barrett's business. To extend your own power."

"My power?" she asked. "What power is it you think I have?"

"You were bedding both rivals," he said. "You picked your side and made your move."

"I was bedding you, too," she said. "Where is that supposed to lead?"

"I don't know."

She stared at him a few moments, then said, "Well, maybe we should find out."

Abruptly, she pulled her shirt out of her skirt, unbuttoned it and dropped it to the floor. There were those glorious breasts again, nipples already hard, smooth flesh dappled with gooseflesh.

"What do you think?" She cupped her big breasts in her own hands and tweaked the nipples with her thumbs.

He thought that he was only a man, after all.

THIRTY-FIVE

Amanda approached him, still holding her breasts in her hands, as if offering them to him. He reached out for them, replacing her hands with his, and lifted them to his mouth. Once again those thick nipples slipped between his lips, his teeth. He chewed and sucked on them while she moaned and held his head. She reached between them to feel his erection through his trousers. He kissed the slopes of her breasts, her neck, her chin and then her lips. She avidly returned the kisses, her head spinning because her memory had not failed her. She was right in thinking that this was the only real man she'd shared a bed with in months—perhaps years.

And now she would share her bed with him.

"Come with me," she said, grabbing his hands.

"I'm going to have to keep my gun close, Amanda," he warned her.

"I'm not going to try to kill you, Clint," she promised with a chuckle, then added, "At least, not until I'm done with you, and that won't be for a long, long time."

He hoped that she was referring to days rather than hours.

• • •

Back at his desk—or the desk he shared with two other inspectors—Callahan was collecting the data Clint had suggested. Both Victor Barrett's organization and Ben Avery's had too many men in them for just him and Clint to face, no matter what Clint's reputation was. And with Captain O'Neal steadfastly refusing to give Callahan any men, they were going to have to come up with a plan—one that would keep them alive.

"Heard you're workin' with a legend of the Old West these days, Charlie," one of the other inspectors said as he passed by.

"Yeah," Callahan started, "it's pretty—"

"Ain't that another way of sayin' you got yourself an old partner?"

The man laughed and walked off.

Idiot, Callahan thought. True, Clint Adams was older than he was, but he was far from old. Working with him had already taught Callahan a lot about dealing with people. This experience would be invaluable to him—unless he ended up losing his job.

Clint Adams was thoroughly enjoying Amanda Tate's heavy breasts, whether the weight of them was in his hands or on his chest. At the moment they were in his face as she sat astride him and rode him. His penis was buried deep in her steamy depths, and as her big breasts swayed in his face, he'd grab them, suck them, lick them—damn, the woman had the most suckable, chewable nipples he'd ever encountered.

She also gave off a fragrance that was a heady mixture of her natural scent, perfume and sex. And because she had a woman's body—all breasts and hips and butt—he enjoyed her entire weight on him. As she would lift her hips up off him and then slam them down, engulfing him again in her heat, the bed would actually leap a couple of inches off the floor.

They grunted and groaned together as they fucked with abandon. There was no love involved in this coupling, just lust and—when he thought about the fact that she had probably killed two people, and maybe more—danger.

But at the moment nobody was thinking about killing anybody—unless having sex with her was going to give him a heart attack. She had a prodigious appetite when it came to sex, and it was all he could do to keep up with her.

But he *was* thinking of death. He was wondering if she enjoyed killing Victor Barrett as much as she had enjoyed having sex with him. This was truly the first time in his life—in his experience with many, many women—that he was with one who might try to kill him when they were done. Amanda was a true black widow.

He felt her slick fluids on his thighs as she continued to ride him, so abruptly he decided to try to assert his superiority. Using all his strength, he heaved himself up and turned the two of them over so that he was on top. He fucked her brutally then, slamming into her again and again, and still she exhorted him to do it harder and harder.

"Give it to me," she cried, "give it all to me, you bastard . . ."

He braced himself, hand on the bed on either side of her, and tried his best to give it to her harder and harder. Then, at one point, it stopped being about her and started being about him, and his own pleasure, his own release. He grunted and groaned and moaned his way to it until they were both crying out, bucking against each other, scratching and clawing and marking each other . . .

THIRTY-SIX

When they were done, Clint quickly rolled away from her to the side of the bed where his gun was hanging from the bedpost. They were both breathing heavily. He had scratches from her nails on his back and arms, and she had welts from his fingers on her pale skin.

"Are you gonna shoot me?" she asked.

"I'm just being careful," he said.

She looked like a wild woman, with her black hair a messy fog around her head, her breasts heaving and nostrils flaring. He found himself wishing there was nothing else between them but the sex. It would have been a hell of a way to spend the rest of the day and night.

"Do you really think I killed Victor Barrett?" she asked. "He was my lover."

"And Ben Avery? Also your lover?"

"Well," she said, "he's young and trainable, and sometimes a gal needs a young lover—don't you think so?"

"I can't comment on that, but he's more than your lover, isn't he?"

"What do you mean?"

"He's your boss."

"My boss?"

"And now, thanks to you, he's ready to take over for Victor Barrett."

Amanda was laughing too hard to answer.

"What's so funny?"

"T-that you t-think B-Ben is my b-boss," she tried to explain. She was laughing so hard her breasts were jiggling.

"Well, if he's not your boss, then what is he?" Clint asked.

She stopped laughing and looked at him seriously.

"If I tell you, you'll leave and never come back," she said. "Or you'll leave and come with the police—but then it would be my word against yours."

"Let's take a chance, Amanda," Clint said. "How about some truth, for a change?"

"Truth," she said, tasting the word. She stood up, walked behind a screen and came back out wearing a long, flimsy robe. It covered her, but she might as well have been naked.

"All right," she said, "let's try it your way. Some truth. But let's do it over a drink. Come with me."

He stood up, pulled on his trousers, strapped on his gunbelt, then carried his boots and shirt as he followed her through the house to another room.

"Have a seat," she said, indicating a maroon divan in the center of the room. There were other chairs in the room that matched it, as did the curtains on the windows.

She went to a sideboard and poured them each a brandy, handed him one.

"I'm sorry, I don't have anything else in the house stronger."

"This is fine."

She sat down in one of the other chairs, crossed her fine legs and then adjusted the robe so that it was covering them.

"I'm going to tell you the truth, Clint, because we're

alone, and because I want your respect. I don't want you thinking of me as a woman who latches onto men."

"I'm ready to hear it," he said.

"You can see that Ben Avery is younger than me," she said. "What you don't know is how much younger. I'm older than I look. So Ben is significantly younger. As for Victor Barrett, he was older than Ben, but still younger than me."

"Okay," Clint said, "I'll accept all that without asking you how old you are."

"I'm at the age now where a man—or boy—younger than Ben might not look at me the way men have always looked at me, might not want me the way men always have."

"I think you've got a lot more years of men wanting you, Amanda."

"You're sweet," she said, sipping her drink. "Actually, Clint, I do latch on to men. I find a man I think has some potential, some talent, and I use him."

"For what?"

"As a front," she said. "You see, neither Victor nor Ben is smart enough to run any kind of operation. And men don't believe that a woman could do it."

"Ah, I think I see where this is going," he said. "You're the woman behind the man."

"Exactly."

"So it's only because of you that Victor Barrett was and Ben Avery is in a position of power."

"Correct."

"What about Ted Singleton?" he asked.

"I didn't know him."

"What?" Clint demanded.

She shrugged. "I just told you I knew him."

"Why?"

"I wanted to talk to you."

"And what about asking me where . . . 'it' was?" he asked her. "What was that about?"

She shrugged. She either didn't know, or she wasn't going to tell him. Either way, he was done with her.

He sipped his drink and set it down on a nearby table unfinished. He pulled on his boots and then donned his shirt.

"Are you leaving?"

"I have to," he said.

"I thought you might."

"Amanda, you're telling me that you run crime organizations through men."

"That's what I'm telling you."

"And obviously, when you have a man like Ben Avery and you want to replace Victor Barrett, you kill the Victor Barretts of your world."

"Let's say, for the sake of argument, that I do that," she said. "What would you do?"

"Well, first I'd leave," he said, "and then I'd tell the police."

"And then you'd have to try and prove that I said it," she said.

"You're probably right," he said, standing up. "I would have to try."

"Clint," she said, quickly leaving her chair. She put her drink down and put her hands on his arms, to stay him. "Why don't you stay with me?"

"Sorry," he said, "I don't relish being the man in front of the woman."

"It wouldn't be like that," she said. "It would be you and me."

"As what?"

"Partners."

"I don't think so, Amanda," he said. "I don't want to run a crime empire. And I don't want to live in a city that has one."

"The Wild West isn't there for you anymore, Clint," she said. "It's time to change."

"You're probably right," he said. "But this isn't the place for me."

"And I'm not the woman for you?" she asked, dropping her hands.

"I'm afraid not."

She undid her robe and allowed it to drop to the floor so she was once again fully naked.

"Are you sure?" she asked, cupping her breasts in her hands. "You can walk away from this?"

"I think I can now, Amanda," he said. "Yes."

He headed for the front door, then turned to look at her again. She was still naked, but she had dropped her hands to her sides.

"Besides," he said, "don't you think I'm a little too old for you?"

THIRTY-SEVEN

When Clint got back to his hotel, it was dark. He found Inspector Callahan waiting for him in the lobby.

"Have you eaten yet?" he asked the younger man.

"No."

"Come on, I'll buy you a steak."

They went into the hotel dining room and ordered two steak dinners.

"What happened?" Callahan asked. "Between you and Amanda Tate?"

Clint told him, leaving out the part where they had sex. He found himself not wanting the young man to think badly of him. So he told him the story, what Amanda had told him about Barrett and Avery.

"Did you believe her?" Callahan asked.

"Actually," Clint said, as the waiter put their dinners in front of them, "I did."

"Nobody else will," Callahan said. "Least of all my bosses. A woman running things? On the docks?"

"I suspect Barrett ran the docks," Clint said, "but he probably did what she told him to do."

"Why would you believe her?"

"Because she's smart," Clint said. "Because she wanted me to know she was smart."

"So you just believe her?"

"Yes."

"How am I supposed to convince anyone of this?"

"Maybe you're not."

"So we . . . what? Ignore it?"

"I haven't got it figured out yet, kid," Clint admitted. "What did you find out?"

"That both Barrett and Avery have—or had—more men than you and I can handle at one time."

"Well, we don't have to worry about Barrett sending any of them after us now, do we?"

"If what Amanda Tate told you is true, maybe she'll send them after us."

"No," Clint said, "they won't listen to her. She's going to have to wait for Avery to swoop in and take control."

"He can't just do that in one day, you know," Callahan said. "Barrett had some men who will resist."

"Did Barrett have any men who might take over for him?"

"Probably not," Callahan said. "Our information is that he had no definite second in command."

"And do you know why that was?"

"Why?"

"Because he was the second in command."

After Clint Adams left her house, Amanda Tate was wondering if she'd done the right thing. If only the man hadn't been so good in bed. If only his legend hadn't made her want him to respect her. True, even if he returned with the police, he couldn't prove she'd said any of the things she'd said, but she may have gotten herself more attention than she wanted.

She got dressed and left the house. She was going to have to get Ben Avery to act faster than she'd first intended.

The tricky part was going to be convincing him it was his idea.

In the past Avery had proved to be controllable. Like most men, she was able to lead him around by his cock. But then he met that Julie Silver and it changed him. Now that Julie was gone, maybe she could get back the control she'd once had.

Maybe just one more big push.

THIRTY-EIGHT

The Docksider Tavern was one of many such taverns on and around the docks. The only thing that distinguished it was the fact that it was owned by Victor Barrett, and he lived upstairs.

The Bucket of Blood was another such tavern. It had nothing to distinguish it from the others, except for the fact that Amanda Tate had just entered. But while she drew glances and admiring looks from the patrons, none made a move toward her, or a comment, because she was known there. She was known as Victor Barrett's woman—but, of course, none of them knew the latest developments in that relationship.

There was another man, however, with whom she had a relationship, the conditions of which no one but they knew. Nine times out of ten he was sitting at a back table by himself, with a bottle of rum and a shot glass. No one spoke to him or even approached him, because the last man who had done so was walking around with one ear.

A woman, however, could approach him, especially a woman like Amanda Tate. And while she had never approached him before, she did now.

She was wearing a wrap, and as she presented herself,

she allowed it to slip to show the swell of her impressive cleavage. She received the response she was looking for. A man will either catch his friend, or wet his lips, and this one did both.

"Well, don't jus' stand there, darlin'," he said, "have you a sit-down."

She pulled a chair out and sat.

"A drink?" he asked.

"I'll have what you're having."

That impressed him. He lifted a hand and the bartender brought over another shot glass. The man poured it full and then refilled his own glass.

"Now, what would be on yer mind, darlin'?"

"You are Kevin O'Donnell?"

"That would be me, yes."

"I understand you kill men for money."

He sipped his rum and studied her, his eyes dwelling on the deepness of her cleavage.

"I do," he said. "I kill people for money. Not just men. You got yerself a woman who's messin' with yer man?" He shrugged.

"That's okay," she said. "I took care of the girl myself."

He raised his eyebrows and sat back.

"Yer an enterprising lady then," he said. "Why do you need me?"

"I need a man killed."

"Are you willin' ta pay?"

"Yes."

"Any price?"

"Within reason."

He looked pointedly at her breasts.

"Yes, even that."

He smiled. He actually had nice, even teeth, and took care of them fairly well. She didn't know how tall he was, but he looked fit, was in his thirties, certainly qualified to be one of her conquests. She only needed him for this one job, though.

"Who do you want killed?"

"First, do you know who I am?"

"I know that yer a fine figure of a woman," he said. "I don't think I've seen yer like in a while."

"I've been in here before."

"Have ya? I guess I didn't notice."

She'd seen him in there a lot, but he rarely looked up from his bottle.

"Do you know who Victor Barrett is?"

"I've heard the name."

"Have you ever done any work for him?"

"From what I heard, he's got his own that does his work for him."

"Well, I have a connection to Victor Barrett. You might hear that from someone in here after I've left. I need you to know that you are dealing with me on this, and no one else."

"Don't want to deal with no one else, darlin'," he said. "Jus' you."

"Good," she said, "then we have that settled."

She drank some of the rum. It was the roughest thing she'd ever had, burned like fire, but she showed nothing to him.

"Ha!" he said, impressed. "Have some more." He topped off her glass. "Now, tell me who it is you'd be havin' me kill."

"His name is Clint Adams." She studied him for a reaction. "Do you know who that is?"

"I do, indeed," he said to her, his eyes glittering, "and I'm thinkin' I'll be wantin' some of my pay up front."

THIRTY-NINE

Over a piece of pie each, Callahan asked, "So with Barrett dead, do we go after Avery?"

"No," Clint said, "we—you, the police—have to go after Amanda. I think she killed Julie, and she killed Barrett. That's what you're concerned with."

"And what are you concerned with?"

"The same thing I have been from the beginning," Clint said. "Finding Ted Singleton, or what happened to him."

"But now you know that Amanda didn't know him."

"I think she's lying," Clint said. "I think Amanda knows everything, and everyone."

"Even what the elusive 'it' is?"

"Especially that, but you know what? I'm the one who doesn't care what it is. I only care about Ted."

"You're not even curious about what these people are chasing?"

Clint shook his head. "Not even curious."

"You're a better man than me," Callahan said. "I'm dying to know what it is."

"Well," Clint said, "whether we want to know or not, I think in the end we might end up finding out."

"But you don't care."

"Not really."

Callahan dropped his knife on his plate and pushed back from the chair.

"Well, to take care of Amanda, I need proof," he said. "Proof, or a confession."

"You know," Clint said, "I could do this the old way."

"The old way meaning the Old West way, when there was no law?"

Clint shrugged.

"You can't just kill her, Clint," Callahan said. "Then I'd be looking for you."

Clint shrugged again.

"Besides," Callahan went on, "she's a woman."

"So?"

"You can't kill a woman."

"She has," Clint said. "She's killed a woman, and a man. She's not playing any favorites, Charlie, why should we?"

"Maybe," Callahan said, "because we're supposed to be the good guys?"

Amanda rolled over and looked down at the sleeping form of Kevin O'Donnell. They were in a run-down shack he called home, on a bed that was hardly more than a pallet. The welts Clint Adams had left on her were still there, but now there was a soreness between her legs she had never experienced before. O'Donnell was easily the most brutal lover she'd ever had. His body was covered with scars—some, he said, earned in his native Ireland, the others here—and he was like no man she had ever been with before. This made him the second such man she had been with this week. But the difference between Clint Adams and Kevin O'Donnell was that the Irishman matched her in temperament. Clint Adams could never live with the things she had done, and the things she would do. Kevin O'Donnell would have no trouble at all.

But she wasn't going to let the Irish killer know that. As

far as he was concerned, this was just the first part of her payment. The next part would be cash, and the last part her body, again. At that time she'd tell him how she felt and see if he felt the same way.

But first they had to get rid of Ben Avery, and then Clint Adams.

FORTY

Clint and Callahan gave it up for the night. The inspector went home and Clint to his room. The next morning Clint had breakfast alone. Something had occurred to him during the night, and he was trying to work it out for himself.

Where was Ted Singleton?

There had not been any sign of him since Clint's arrival in Sacramento. Both Julie Silver and Amanda Tate claimed to have been working with him. Amanda claimed to have lied about it, and Clint hadn't believed her when she said it. Now he wasn't so sure. And what about Julie? What reason could she have had to lie?

Clint took out again the telegram that he had received from Singleton, and read it. There was nothing in the wording that helped him. But why had the United States government been mentioned by both Julie and Amanda?

Clint finally decided that after breakfast it was time for him to send a telegram of his own.

Clint stopped off at the telegraph office to send another telegram to Washington. He was wondering now who was lying, one of the two women or Washington? Jim West

165

may not have been able to admit that there was some sort of operation going on in Sacramento. Maybe if he knew that Singleton was involved—Clint's first telegram had not mentioned that—the answer might be different.

When Clint entered, the key operator quickly jumped to his feet.

"I didn't say nothin'!" he snapped.

"Relax," Clint said. "I just wanted to send another one."

"Oh, o-okay."

"And you won't have to worry about passing this one on to Victor Barrett. He's dead."

"Really?"

"Yes," Clint said. "You'll have to find yourself another little sideline."

"Uh, n-no," the clerk said. "I learned my lesson. I ain't doin' that no more."

"Good for you." Clint wrote down his message and passed it to the clerk. This time he wasn't so worried about his wording, except in one place. He actually told West that Singleton was missing, and had claimed to be working for "him" in D.C.

"Will you want the reply brought to the same place?" the clerk asked.

"Yes, and as soon as possible."

"Yes, sir."

Clint paid the man and left. By the time he got back to his hotel, Inspector Callahan was waiting.

"Where've you been?" Callahan asked.

"Were you worried?"

"Well, yes," the younger man said. "I don't need to have you turn up missing, like your friend."

"Yes, I've been thinking about that."

"Thinking about what?"

"Let me ask you," Clint said, "what if Ted was never here?"

"At the hotel?"

"No," Clint said, patiently. "What if he never was in Sacramento?"

"Then who sent you the telegram, and why?"

"Yep," Clint said, "those would be the questions we're left with, all right."

"That's something we don't need," Callahan said, "more questions."

"Well, there's something else I should tell you," Clint said. He looked around. "Come over here," he said, and led Callahan to a sofa in the lobby. It was still early and they had the lobby to themselves.

Clint had decided to tell Callahan about the possible involvement of the Secret Service. He'd decided that he trusted the honest young policeman.

Callahan listened patiently, his eyes growing wider and wider.

"Why didn't you tell me before?" Callahan demanded when Clint was done.

"In my past dealings with the Secret Service I've always had to be . . . well, secretive."

Callahan's eyes got even wider.

"You've worked for the United States Secret Service?" he asked.

"With," Clint said, "I've worked with them. I have a good friend who's an agent. We help each other out from time to time."

"Have you asked your friend if Julie or Amanda's claims are legitimate?"

"I sent a telegram when I first talked to them. The response was that there were no agents in this area."

"But?"

"Well, now I'm wondering if they were just covering," Clint finished. "So I sent another, more specific telegram this morning. Hopefully, this reply will tell us something."

"This is just more confusing for me," Callahan said, shaking his head.

"How are things at headquarters?"

"You can't believe how many people are upset about Barrett's death," Callahan said. "I didn't realize how many policemen he had on his payroll. It's very . . . disappointing."

"Maybe now that Barrett's dead things will change," Clint suggested.

"And what if Ben Avery just takes over? Picks up where Barrett left off. How can I keep working in a department that's so corrupt?"

"I don't know, Charlie," Clint said. "Have you talked to your friend, the lieutenant? Is he one of the clean ones?"

"I've always thought so," Callahan said, "but how can I be sure?" He shook his head. "I've got a good mind just to turn in my badge and leave Sacramento. Do something else."

"Like what? Join another police department?"

"Maybe," Callahan said, "maybe in the East."

"Do you really think they'll be less corrupt?" Clint asked.

"I could only hope so," Callahan said, and then his eyes widened again, this time for a different reason. "Hey, what about the Secret Service?"

"You want to work for the Secret Service?"

"Why not? You know people there. You could get me an interview."

"Charlie—"

"Unless you think they're corrupt, too?"

"There's probably a certain amount of corruption no matter where you go," Clint said, "but I think the Service is probably one of the cleaner law enforcement agencies."

"Then what do you say?" Callahan asked. "Can you arrange that for me?"

"Charlie, why don't we wait until we're done here?"

Clint suggested. "Let's finish what we started, and then we'll go from there."

"Well . . . I suppose you're right. I guess I should finish. But then we'll talk about the Secret Service?"

"Yes," Clint said, "then we'll talk about it."

FORTY-ONE

"Don't you think he'll be suspicious?" O'Donnell asked.

"Yes," Amanda said, "of course he will . . . but he'll come anyway."

"You're sure?"

"Dead sure."

"Yer an amazin' woman, Amanda," O'Donnell said.

"I'm just hoping that you're an amazing man," Amanda said. "Do you know somebody who can deliver this note to his hotel?"

"Jus' leave it with me, darlin'," the killer said, "I'll take care of it."

In the harsh light of morning Amanda could see that O'Donnell's shack was a pigsty. Amanda decided she'd have to take him out of there once the job was done. If she was going to be seen with him, he'd have to be cleaned up, too. And she'd have to buy him some new clothes.

"Now remember, dear," she said to the Irishman, "he's the Gunsmith. He's very good with a gun."

"Well," O'Donnell said, "so am I."

"I thought your weapon was a knife."

"Knife, gun, baling hook," O'Donnell said. "I can use them all. Don't you worry."

She stood up from the pallet and looked down at her new man and lover. A bath wouldn't have hurt him, either. And maybe a haircut and a shave.

"I'll see you tonight then," she said.

"You're sure you want to be there?"

"I wouldn't miss it," she said. She leaned down and kissed him. As she started away, he grabbed her arm and held on.

"Aren't ya forgettin' somethin', lass?"

She stared at him.

"The second part of my payment," he said. "I might have to hire on a couple of lads, you know. Just in case he brings a friend?"

"Actually," she said, "he might have a policeman with him."

"Whoa, there," he said. "That might cost extra."

She took his chin in her hand and said, "I think we can think up something extra for you."

"I meant money," he said. "Gelt, coin?"

"I have money," she said. She opened her bag, took out a sheaf of bills and passed it over.

"You got lots of this?" he asked, after a whistle.

"Lots."

"Well," he said, "make sure you bring some tonight. We'll pay off the boys I use and then celebrate. Eh?"

"Celebrating sounds good," she said.

After she left, he sat back and counted the money she'd handed him, his eyes growing wide, a warmth spreading through his body.

Clint and Callahan decided there was nothing better for them to do than wait around the hotel for the reply to the telegram. They sat together on chairs out in front of the hotel.

Clint told Callahan what Washington, D.C., was like, as the young man had asked. Clint didn't know if Callahan was Secret Service material, but he saw no harm in telling him about the wonders of the nation's capital.

"Are there pretty women there?" Callahan asked.

"There are pretty women here, Charlie. I've seen them."

"I've heard that women from the East are prettier than women from the West."

"Well, I've been both places and in between, and I'm here to tell you there are pretty women all over."

They talked a bit more about places Clint had been, and then they spotted the telegraph operator coming their way.

"Here's that reply you wanted, Mr. Adams." The clerk held it out and then quickly turned and walked away when Clint accepted it.

"What's it say?"

"It says a few things," Clint said, "and none of them help."

"Like what?"

Clint folded it and tucked it into his pocket.

"There are no Secret Service agents in this area," Clint said. "There haven't been for months."

"And what else?"

"This is the one that really doesn't help me."

"Don't keep me in suspense."

"According to my friend Jim," Clint said, "Ted Singleton died several years ago."

"What?"

"That's right," Clint said, "so he couldn't have sent me a telegram asking me to meet him here."

"Then who did?"

"That's the question."

FORTY-TWO

They were still sitting there, contemplating the latest information, when a man dressed in dirty street clothes, not wearing a gun, approached.

"One of you Clint Adams?" he asked.

"That's me."

"I got somethin' for ya." The man took out a piece of paper, but didn't hand it over. "Lady said you'd gimme the price of a drink if I delivered it."

"Listen, you—"

"It's okay, Charlie," Clint said. He took out a couple of coins. "Here you go, friend. Get two drinks."

"Wow! Thanks." The man handed over the note and then took off running to the nearest saloon.

"Take a look," Clint said, after reading it.

Callahan read it, then looked at Clint.

"This is the docks," he said. "You know this is a trap."

"Sure it is."

"She's setting you up to be killed."

"And you can arrest her for it," Clint said.

"It says come 'alone.' "

"Well," Clint said, "going with you, I consider that alone."

"Gee, thanks."

• • •

The appointment to meet Amanda Tate was not until after
dark. Even further indication that it was a trap. Clint and
Callahan talked about getting some men to back them up,
but the inspector told Clint that the captain was determined
not to give them any help.

"Then we'll go it alone," Clint said. "Let's put it to rest
tonight."

Clint went down to the docks alone, confident that
Callahan would find a way to be there. What he wasn't sure
about was whether Amanda would be there or not.

But she was. She was standing at the end of the dock,
wrapped in some kind of a cape. He wondered if she'd
have a gun of her own, or if she'd leave it to others to do
the dirty deed.

"Clint," she said, "you came."

"That's right, Amanda," he said. "I want it all to end here."

"So do I," she said. "I'm sorry, but that's the way it has
to be."

"Tell me why you killed Julie Silver."

She shrugged. "She was in my way. Ben had fallen for
her, and I wasn't done with him yet."

"Did she really know Ted Singleton?" he asked. "Or a
man who claimed to be Singleton?"

"I told you," she said. "I never knew Singleton. I just
told you that. I needed to know what you were doing in
Sacramento."

"Why?"

"Because you're a man with a rep," she said. "If someone here hired you, I needed to know. I have people in all
the hotels feeding me information. When I heard you were
there, I came."

"You mentioned Singleton."

"No, you did," she said, "when you mentioned Julie."

Damn it, he couldn't remember. Was she still lying,
even though she intended to kill him?

"And what was everyone chasing, Amanda?" he asked. "What was the 'it' you and Julie asked me about?"

"To tell you the truth, I don't know that, either," she said. "I don't think there was anything. I think somebody fed Julie a line and she fell for it."

"Wait a minute," he said. "You fed her that line. You made her think there was something of value—"

"I don't have time for this, Clint."

"What about Barrett?"

"Oh, you know I killed him," she said. "I had to get rid of him."

Clint hoped Callahan was close enough to hear.

"What now, Amanda?"

"I'm sorry, Clint," she said. "You're a delicious man, but no sex tonight. Only dying."

Suddenly, he heard a sound behind him, and turned to see four men coming toward him. They were carrying clubs and knives. He didn't see a gun.

"Oh, goddamn it!" Amanda snapped.

Obviously, this wasn't what she had been expecting, but Clint didn't have time to see what she was doing. The men were advancing on him with bad intentions.

He drew his gun and they stopped.

"What the fuck—" one of them said. "There wasn't supposed to be no gun."

"What do we do?" another asked.

"Let's get 'im anyway," a third said, harshly. "He can't shoot all of us."

Quickly, Clint shot that man in the knee. He howled and went down, clutching his bloodied leg.

"Hold it!" someone shouted from the dark.

Just as suddenly as the four toughs had appeared, Callahan was there with his friend, Lieutenant Powell. Both had guns in their hands.

"Drop your weapons!" Powell shouted, and the men obeyed.

Clint turned quickly to see where Amanda was, but she was gone. Had she gone into the water? He hadn't heard a splash. A boat? Maybe.

He turned as Callahan reached him.

"You all right?" the inspector asked.

"I'm fine. Did you hear her confess? To killing them both?"

Callahan looked sheepish. "I didn't get here in time. I managed to convince Lieutenant Powell to come along, but we got here too late. I'm sorry, Clint. I didn't hear her."

Clint ejected the spent shell from his gun, reloaded and holstered it.

"All right," he said. "Let's see who sent these fellas after me."

FORTY-THREE

When Amanda got to O'Donnell's shack, she barged in
without knocking. He was there, on the bed with a skinny
blond whore.

"What the hell—" she said. "Where were you?"

He rolled over and looked at her without concern.

"Whataya mean?"

"You were supposed to be on the dock. You were supposed to kill Clint Adams."

"I was supposed to see to it that he died," O'Donnell
said. "I never said I was gonna do it meself, ya daft
woman. You got the rest of me money?"

"Money? I'm not giving you any more money. In fact, I
want my money back. And what are you doing with her?"

"What's it look like I'm doin', ya stupid whore? I'm
fookin' 'er."

"You're supposed to be with me."

"Ya think one roll in me sheets means ya own me? Yer
stupider than I thought."

"Give me back my money, you bastard!" she snapped.

"Pay me what you owe me, ya whore!"

Suddenly, her hand went into her bag so quickly he
knew it wasn't for money. He sprang naked off the bed and

got to her before she could get the small gun out. He slapped her, took her bag and knocked her down, then he dug the gun out. The skinny whore, flat-chested but with great big brown nipples, watched from the bed with wide eyes.

"Stupid woman," he said. "You were gonna shoot me with this?" He dug into her bag again, then came out with another sheaf of money like the first one. He'd paid those four dockworkers twenty dollars each to kill Clint Adams, not caring if they got the job done or not, and kept the remainder of the money. Now he had the same amount again. He was rich. Time to leave.

"You can't—" Amanda said from the floor. She was furious. "You belong with me. We were going to—"

He pointed the little gun at her, and before she could say another word, he shot her between the eyes. She died with a look of amazement on her face.

"Oh my God!" the whore on the bed said.

O'Donnell turned and looked at her.

"I won't say nothin', Kevin," the girl said. "I promise."

He walked to the bed and pointed the gun at her.

"I can't leave ya behind, Belinda, darlin'," he said. "Sorry."

"Take me with you," she said, in a flash of clarity. "I need to get away from here. So do you. I'll be good to you, Kevin. I don't want your money. Just get me out of here."

He cocked the gun, studied her young, pretty face. Younger by far than that stupid cow on the floor. She thought after one fuck he was going to be in her thrall? Not Kevin O'Donnell, no sir.

He eased the hammer back down on the gun.

"Okay, then," he said to the whore, Belinda. "Get dressed, darlin'. We're away!"

• • •

A couple of hours later, when Clint Adams, Inspector Callahan and Lieutenant Powell entered the shack and found Amanda on the floor, O'Donnell was long gone.

"Looks like our missing friend didn't honor his part of the deal," Powell said.

Clint picked up her bag and went through it. For the most part it was empty. On the bed was a small gun that would have fit in the bag.

"Gun on the bed," he said.

Callahan picked it up.

"Been fired."

"Probably the one that did the job," Powell said. "Looks like your case is solved, kid."

"She killed Julie Silver and Victor Barrett," Clint said. "I'll sign a statement to that effect."

"I'll get some men in here to clean up," Powell said, and left.

"So it's over?" Callahan asked.

"It's over."

"But it doesn't make any sense," he said. "None of it."

"It doesn't have to make sense all the time, Charlie," Clint said.

"B-but . . . Singleton . . . the telegram . . . whatever they were all after . . ."

"Unanswered questions," Clint said.

"But . . . no answers?"

"Okay, try this," Clint said. "Somebody knew that I was friends with Ted Singleton a long time ago. They also knew the police department here was corrupt. Maybe Singleton told that somebody a while ago that I was a good man to have on his side. So this somebody sends me a telegram, signs Ted's name, figuring I'll come to the aid of a friend. And while I'm here, I help clean some things up."

"Like what?"

"Barrett, Amanda," Clint said.

"We still got Avery," Callahan said. "And we still have corrupt policemen."

"You have to go a step at a time, Charlie."

"What about that other thing we were talking about?" Callahan asked.

"The Secret Service?" Clint asked. "I can talk to somebody, Charlie, but do you really want to leave here? With a job half-done?"

"What can I do to clean it all up?"

"You alone? Maybe nothing. But somebody sent me that telegram. You've got somebody here who cares. Maybe your friend Powell?"

"You think he sent the telegram?"

"I'm just saying somebody did," Clint said, "which means you're not alone."

Callahan scratched his head.

"I guess you're right."

"Keep doing your job, Charlie," Clint said. "I'll talk to somebody in Washington, and one day you may get the call. But until then, just keep being the best policeman you can be."

"And what are you gonna do?"

"Same thing I always do," Clint said. "I'll go on being the best me I can be. See, that's a job I do well."

Watch for

SHADOW WALKER

304th novel in the exciting GUNSMITH series
from Jove

Coming in April!

GIANT ACTION! GIANT ADVENTURE!

THE GUNSMITH

GIANT

Giant Westerns featuring The Gunsmith

LITTLE SURESHOT AND THE WILD WEST SHOW
0-515-13851-7

DEAD WEIGHT
0-515-14028-7

RED MOUNTAIN
0-515-14206-9

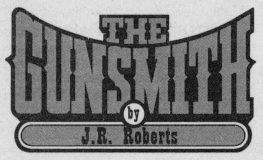